Tragedy of Fear

"Vietnam, the unwinnable war and graveyard of the mighty."

Edward Harris

Edward Harris (signature)

TRAGEDY OF FEAR

In Absolute Secrecy

to Terry who kindly helps me to hear. (handwritten inscription)

FAIRFIELD PRESS

Distributed by Gazelle Book Services Limited
Hightown, White Cross Mills, South Rd, Lancaster
England LA1 4XS

British Library Cataloguing in Publication Data
A catalogue record for this book is available from the British
Library

ISBN 0-9546415-0-7

Typeset by Amolibros, Milverton, Somerset
This book production has been managed by Amolibros
Printed and bound by Advance Book Printing, Oxford, England

DEDICATION

*This book is dedicated to every
David with a sling-shot and guts*

CONTENTS

About the Author

EDWARD HARRIS WAS born in North London and educated by the Church of England, his mother hoping for a priest in the family. Higher studies were private with a retired Oxford don and friend of the family, who encouraged reading of the classics.

Disinclined to the priesthood, preferring the business world, he went first to Pitmans, then to Clark's Colleges. This led to a partnership in a small chemical company, which was mothballed when war came.

He volunteered for the army, becoming a Territorial, Officer Training and a King's Commission. He spent eight years' service overseas in the Western Desert, in Burma, and in Indo-China in Intelligence. He was placed on Reserve of Officers, retiring when fifty-five.

In Malaya after the war he managed a motor company branch office and found a flare for writing and journalism. He was recalled from reserve to active duty to assist with his knowledge of security intelligence, during the Chinese Emergency in 1950.

Chance took him to the Bahamas where he pioneered putting electricity into a part of Eleuthera, an out island, where he lived for sixteen years, developing tourism and freelance journalism. His bus service, covering the whole island 100 miles long, gave mobility to all settlements with a chance for boy to meet girl of far away, and romance to blossom.

He retired to New Zealand when seventy, but returned to England for family reasons where he spends time writing articles for the press.

My thanks to Greta Lewis, a friend who made it happen.

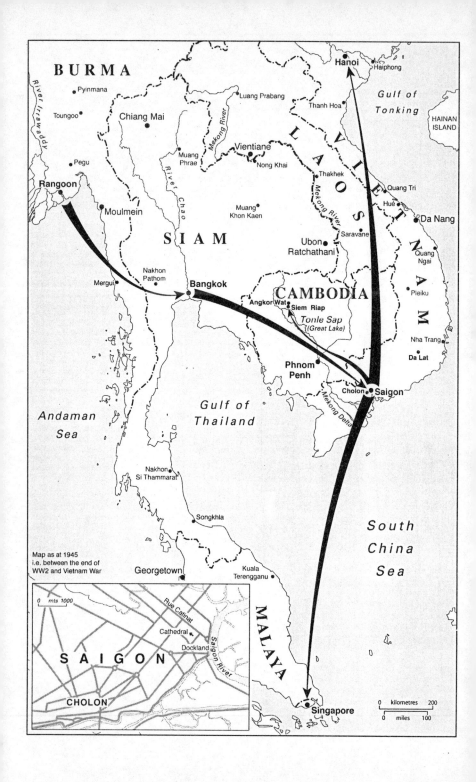

PROLOGUE

EIGHTH MAY 1945, a momentous date in history. Europe—
now at peace after four and a half years of madness, sadness
and the stench of death—fell quiet, the guns silent.

German surrender was accepted by the Allies. Rejoicing
in European capitals is tinged and muted in the knowledge
that yet another foe has to be conquered in the Orient; a
war-weary world's burden to be borne until victory in the
East is won.

Focus now on the Pacific, Americans raid the beaches
of Iwo Jima and Okinawa, in bloody battle against the
fanatical and unpredictable Japanese of Pearl Harbor infamy.

By June these victories are secure, enabling the USA
to be in striking distance of the Japanese mainland.

At this juncture Russia plans to enter the Japanese war,
giving moral and psychological support to the Americans.

Bombing raids together with naval blockades begin to
weaken the Japanese population. War is nearing its end
but heavy costs in men and materials must be incurred
to secure the peace.

Soviet, British and American heads of state meet in
conference with other Allied leaders at the imposing vine-

clad Cecilienhof Palace in Potsdam, an unbombed suburb of Berlin, as prelude to the mammoth task of reclaiming, resettling, restoring and re-governing lands in turmoil.

The Potsdam Conference started on 17th July lasting until 2nd August, with reconstruction and aid plans giving succour and practical help to countries devastated by war.

Fifteen leading statesmen, both military and political— including Winston Churchill (three days later Clement Atlee took his place, as the Tories were voted out of office), Joseph Stalin and Harry S Truman—crowded with mean elbowroom at a round table, their advisers serving busily behind them.

Together they hammered at the numerous problems in reoccupation of territories in enemy hands... not quickly or easily. Thunderous and at times ugly voices, accompanied by clenched fists pounding the air, gave forceful meaning to points of principle.

Geographical importance of Indo-China, where a confused political situation prevailed, required special attention. To allow an uncontrolled communist regime to take over would pose a threat to the whole of the Far East, thus menacing Australia and New Zealand. A strong independence movement under the communist Ho Chi-minh had been created, assisted by the Japanese—with an eye to future beneficial trade relations.

Naturally the French—as the former colonial power— wanted sole control. This was deemed by some to be a recipe for disaster. Anyway, Ho Chi-minh would never accept, and turmoil must result, possibly amounting to war of unlimited duration with an aftermath of enormous proportions; it was never an option, in the eyes of the British contingent.

But, options were few and enormously difficult to implement. Heated argument ensued, voices were raised. Eventually these victorious World War II Allies finally came to the inevitable compromise... they played for time.

After much bickering it is concluded that, as British troops are available for instant deployment, Britain be requested to appoint a military head of mission for Indo-China.

Historians will come to believe that something resembling a conspiracy was used to persuade France to reclaim Indo-China part of the French Union.

Major-General Douglas Gracey, veteran of war in Burma, known for his tenacity of purpose, was chosen by his old regimental pal General William Slim, now general officer commanding all Allied forces in South East Asia.

Gracey, a strong-minded man and successful fighting general, with his 20th Indian Division, comprising Indian and Gurkha troops, had a notable record of success in defeating the Japanese in Burma. Slim selected him for this tricky job mainly because his division was still intact and ready for the move from Rangoon to Saigon with minimum problems of organisation.

Gracey was known to possess the rugged qualities needed to deal with the mixture of peoples and circumstances prevailing in what used to be called French Indo-China. He would be assisted by a professional Foreign Office expert, leaving him free to deal with military aspects and providing an interim administration until the chiefs-of-staff meeting at Potsdam decided on the future government most suitable for the territory.

Some political and military minds may view Gracey's appointment as a means for France to become the boss again. He was rumoured to love empires governed by white men. For this reason he would be a popular choice to the French whose colony Indo-China had been before the war.

Major-General Gracey arrived in Singapore from Rangoon, full of himself and all fired up for his briefing by Admiral Mountbatten—Supreme Allied Commander, South East Asia.

It was the French flavour that appealed: Gracey liked the French and was known to be sympathetic to their return as colonial master. He, already attuned to the possibility of influencing this outcome, found it disconcerting to hear Admiral Mountbatten's severe stricture against any involvement in political affairs of any kind. He felt immediately deflated; his ego blunted, his dream of playing a man of influence abashed. He shrank in stature and importance; he had pictured himself as the man of the moment, in the twilight of his military career.

Admiral Mountbatten told him forcibly that Britain must not be seen to favour any one nation in the choice of government for Indo-China. Britain's future relations with whoever was appointed must appear neutral. It was more than likely that split responsibilities would be preferred. This might include Ho Chi-minh's party. Partition was on the cards with Ho in the north and the French in the south.

Gracey's preconceived ideas now needed revision. He thought of the scene with Ho's communist influence in the north aided by Chinese sympathisers just over the border supplying arms and economic support; the French in the south providing and maintaining a costly defence force permanently: it would never work. As a strong colonialist he saw an impossible situation and decided that the USA would favour the restoration of France as a bulwark against communism. All would be well in the end, without his influence, he decided.

What he did not realise was that France was even now moving quickly to a socialist state, very strongly to the left.

$\mathcal{L}$

A crestfallen Major-General Gracey arrived back at General Slim's HQ, who was just then placing the phone down and obviously very angry. Not easily impassioned and demonstrative, Slim showed the telltale signs of extreme displeasure when aroused.

Shocked by the face of a man he thought he knew so well as a close friend, Gracey was disturbed. General Slim stared at him with a kind of snarl; his anger displayed by the drumming of fingers on the highly polished rosewood desk.

Mountbatten was on the phone, tearing strips off Slim for recommending Gracey for this job. What made Gracey question Mountbatten's orders forbidding him to play politics? Mountbatten was, after all, speaking for the Allied Chiefs of Staff. Gracey had been very foolish and might have been sacked, but for the fact that he was the only commander with troops ready to go to Indo-China.

General Slim was able to mollify the situation and agreed to give Gracey a severe reprimand.

A contrite and humbled major-general had thought it necessary to get one or two points clear with Admiral Mountbatten because, as he saw things, politics would play an important part in this job. Much more so, he thought, in relations between communism and capitalism.

General Slim, his fist hitting the desk with force, reminded Gracey that politics plays a part in war… but not for army generals. True, he agreed, this task was different from a battlefield situation and here diplomacy played a very important part, but it was not for the military to get involved.

Politics is always part of the cause and the outcome; the solution rests with politicians.

The Supreme Allied Commander had to ensure that politics played no part in the military responsibility of providing law and order until a final decision was agreed, as to the future government of the country. This must be left to someone else. Gracey felt the sting of this dressing down.

Urgency had been Major-General Gracey's perpetual problem for many months. Commanding his 20th Indian Division against both the jungle terrain of Burma and a fanatical Japanese enemy, he had urgency and alertness as constant companions in every situation; particularly towards the end of the Burma campaign, which became "the race to Rangoon", necessitating quick thinking and snap decisions based, as always, on sound military judgement.

In these conditions he had no one to consult; every decision was his to make—right or wrong.

He had approached this job in the same way, forgetting that political policy was not of his making, in this difficult and delicate situation.

General Slim explained that he had to know all that was going on, both on and under the table. The general looked askew to see if Gracey had recovered his poise and told him of the most important consideration, the security intelligence set-up. Everyone, he explained, would be on the make in one form or another. The problem would be to know friend from foe. Intrigue would abound with commies of all brands doing their damnedest to prevent the re-establishment of French or any Western control of the country.

The Americans, too, would have fancy ideas, he explained, with their Office of Strategic Services (OSS) exercising their powerful, sinister influence. Things would be very difficult without the right eyes and ears to see what was going on.

General Slim carried on revealing other areas of importance such as that of expatriate Chinese who, pre-war, controlled most of the internal commerce of the country. No one knew how they would fare or how they would see their future, or what plans they had to influence events.

The general knew of no place in a society of extreme nationalist persuasion for Chinese nationals or those of other countries; particularly if a policy of ethnic cleansing was enforced.

General Slim pointed out that this job was dangerous and exciting, calling for greatest care when dealing with both native people and those of other interested countries such as France and the USA.

Major-General Gracey needed to know how Admiral Mountbatten expected a soldier to sort this lot out. He felt it right to suggest that a diplomat from the Foreign Office might be found to deal with the obviously sensitive elements of this very involved mission.

On this score General Slim was able to satisfy him.

A specialist was found named Peter Bain, a fluent French speaker with a Parisian wife. He had been highly successful in other places and was considered right for this assignment.

On the security intelligence side of things, Gracey naturally was concerned that the requirement called for, as he put it, a superman. He doubted if such a person existed and asked for proof that this responsible position would be satisfactorily filled.

General Slim assured him that a most suitably qualified officer had been found, a Major Andrew Grant who was, until recently, part of the army headquarters' intelligence team.

Grant was first discovered in Rangoon in 1942. General Slim was then visiting the beleaguered 7th Armoured Brigade, when Grant, a tank commander, challenged a Burman climbing onto a British tank; Grant spoke Burmese—something unusual in an officer having no pre-war association with Burma.

General Slim again came across the same man in Delhi, in 1944, where he was on an advanced intelligence course. The general chatted with him, discovering that Major Grant knew a great deal about Indo-China having operated clandestine forays into Cambodia and Laos. It was then that he decided to join the general's intelligence team.

Grant was now at the Military Intelligence School in Matlock, Derbyshire, training commissioned and non-commissioned officers for service in Indo-China, and General Slim suggested that Gracey took a week's leave in England to find out if there was mutuality between him and Andrew Grant.

1

A PRODUCT OF powerful Highland stock going back to the days of clan warfare, I'd already spent much of my time operating clandestine networks of spies, saboteurs and agents throughout the Far East. My qualifications for preparing specialist officers are impeccable; but I'm better doing it for real, not in the classroom! I'm essentially one to whom bespoke killing has become my chosen covert occupation... in certain circumstances.

I'd been withdrawn from special duty in Indo-China by devious means and attached to the School of Military Intelligence in Matlock, Derbyshire, for sinister purposes. My cover was to prepare selected commissioned and non-commissioned officers for extraordinary duties in final operations against the Japanese. This posting had not been officially recorded.

The school, housed in a pre-war health hydro, made no pretence at being beautiful; probably the ugliest building I'd ever seen, but with enough functional, self-contained facilities for staff and students to live and work comfortably.

My lecture had finished and students were departing, as Lance Corporal Armstrong made his way to my lectern.

"The commandant asks if you'll report to him, soon as you're free from this session, sir," was spoken in the soft Perthshire dialect, reminding me of my mother I'd not seen for two years.

I'd been warned by Singapore to expect a visit by a Major-General Gracey who was forming a military commission for Indo-China. I nodded assent while gathering up my notes and wondering if this was it.

✑

"The commandant's waiting for you, sir," smiled the woman army corporal, who seemed more than usually friendly, even intimate. She wore that wonderful look of desire in her eyes that women unintentionally reveal at special moments.

The brigadier commandant I'd met on arrival was a small, pleasant man of sharp features, ruddy complexion, sporting a neatly trimmed moustache; he stood up, as did his guest, a large man, his tunic ablaze with medal ribbons of both world wars.

"Ah, Andrew," beamed the commandant. "Thank you for coming so quickly. It will be good if you can spare an hour of your time." Turning to Major-General Gracey he continued, with a touch of pride, "Here he is, general. Major Grant."

We talked alone for a full hour, the brigadier having left us. The general explained in detail the nature of the assignment, its problems and the purpose of the commission in Indo-China. "Our task is to take over the day-to-day running of government, confining the Japs to barracks. We are a military control, applying such laws as are required to maintain order. In particular, we have to stay out of politics, as ordered by the Allied Chiefs of Staff."

My impression of him was mixed, man to man: I saw a battlefield soldier of powerful determination but no subtlety.

Listening intently and wanting answers to specific questions, I began liking the idea of being involved in this potentially exciting phase of post-war reconstruction, in familiar surroundings of former guerrilla activities. My experience of the region during Japanese occupation told of the numerous factions in existence, some militant groups fully armed and well trained, who would create their own special kind of problems. I was thrilled and excited, going back where I belong; I could now come alive, in action at last with my field-security sections.

Major-General Gracey had the confidential file, which covered every part of my army service, with reports on each mission, secret and otherwise. It detailed my secondment to Force 136: covert operations behind enemy lines in Burma and Indo-China. This revealed my toughness and dedication; and my languages: French, Japanese and Mandarin. Intimate knowledge of local customs and politics and a readymade network of agents throughout Indo-China, made me perfect for the job.

"Is this up your street, major?" asked the general, who must have known what my reply would be, having been briefed by General Slim.

Adding to my already new-found excitement, a smile spread across my face as, with classic junior-officer audacity, I replied slowly: "General, I think you very well know, it is *precisely* my street!"

We both laughed.

Speed of preparation is vital. I've got three weeks to produce a special unit. Space in the school's annexe is provided, to get things started, with the able assistance of a tough-looking army woman, driver-cum-clerk, the type that always knows exactly where and from whom to get things. Less lecturing for me, but enough to justify my being on the staff.

My needs of people and equipment were paramount. First, I wanted Paul Hunter in quickly—his unique skills and expertise made him prime choice as organiser. I knew Captain Hunter well in Burma and the North African desert where he ran a tailor-made brand of field security section. Now, chief instructor at the School of Military Intelligence, Karachi, speaking fluent French, Japanese and Hockien, with some Burmese—languages vital to the job.

He reported rapidly following my urgent request to General Headquarters, Delhi and together, wasting no time, we formed a skeleton organisation; within twenty-four hours there was flesh on the bones.

"We need another like you, Paul, someone with your special brand of cunning, speaking French and some dialect of Chinese. Maybe one of your former students?"

"Stafford May!" said Hunter with alacrity. "Just the man we need. Also speaks French and Thai fluently and some Annamese. Don't know where he is now. Last saw him in Hong Kong on a hush-hush job."

"Good enough." I lifted the phone.

Captain May was quickly traced, to, of all places, the School of Oriental Languages in London, teaching French.

Kathie, our first-class forager-cum-clerk, looks up

approvingly as Stafford May enters her small outer office. She's decided that with this handsome man in the unit her interests will need careful watching. She was definitely impressed.

"Hallo," he smiles, "I'm Stafford May, reporting to Major Grant. Is this the right place?"

Kathie grins back, "Yes, sir. I'll tell him you're here."

Between us, using all resources of mind and memory, Hunter, May and I pieced together two sections, each of fifteen handpicked men skilled in a variety of cunning and disciplines: one team for Hunter, the other for May.

The "bodies", as the thirty were called, came from various walks of life—all were special.

To the professional regulars, our work is second nature; to others, particularly the conscript soldiers, it is something else: the Oxford don discovers inner qualities of daring and unsuspected desires for excitement; while the garage owner and a solicitor experience revelations of personal strengths beyond expectations. Over all, men became total beings stretched to limits they would have thought impossible. Professionals from MI5 and Special Branch were the perfect bonding ingredient, forming the core others attached to; they're now blokes, not gents. Movements and speech become faster—more precise and urgent.

By the end of the second week I've got a tough and fully qualified unit possessing the skills in languages, techniques and the disreputable business of obtaining information by any means, any way. Very special radio equipment, hand-made-to-measure of light-weight materials, small and easily concealed, created by one genius in our unit.

Word came for us to report to Poole in Dorset. A final conference was arranged quickly. Using a giant model of Saigon City our operatives were familiarised with the geography of the place; particularly locations of agents who would provide both initial and future intelligence.

To Hunter—tall and blond, of broad shoulders with narrow hips—already enjoying this briefing, it meant action was not far away. He laughed rudely at one of my jokes and remarked, "I like it. When do we move off? Did you say two days?"

Stafford May, dark of hair, bronzed, not so tall but much more athletic, replied, "Yes, pal. Only two more days and we're off to the land of mystery and intrigue. And, I hope, luscious Annamite lovelies."

With rare exceptions this unit, comprising men of varying ages from twenty-four to thirty-six, all of different social backgrounds, had harmony and *esprit de corps* of rare quality. As though, because of their natural intelligence, they spoke the same intellectual language of respect. Each could hold his own without fear of being outsmarted; each, in his own way, was special—essential to the well-being of the whole. Failure of two unfortunates I'd parted with was personality problems—the boffin type: very intelligent and skilled in their field, proved more mouse than man: no good in the extreme situations of Indo-China, where death lurks without warning, and a sixth sense is imperative.

Looking at the end result I feel smug and satisfied, a rather superior attitude. We have produced a splendid team of thirty tough, hard, intelligent men, who've changed out of all recognition to their former civilian selves. They've made their own jargon as a bonding agent, giving them confidence with a touch of arrogance.

Strategic associations and friendships develop between these diverse types; Benoit, the dusky Grenadian policeman from the West Indies, for example, found a friend in Carrysfort, the Oxford don. Probably, more their differences than anything else made this possible, in these unique conditions. Each had strong affiliations with other members of the team—a brotherhood.

Growing comradeship with Hunter and May, valuable in my job, made decisions on policy and planning mutually agreed without fuss. There was one other task before the leave break: my two section commanders required final briefing... there were things needing careful explanation.

"Those essential to us at the start of things are Eddie Blitz and Maryse Boulay de la Meurthe. I'll contact them soon after arrival. The next is Cheong Sie-ling. Study the files, memorise and destroy. Cheong Sie-ling, by the way, is very special since he handles the Chinese factor which must influence the outcome. His codename is "Slippery", as you will discover, he's like an eel mentally—very hard to catch out. Many have tried and failed!"

Now we can relax. With the sun still high and the evening balmy, Paul, Stafford and I set out to spend our twenty-four-hour leave in London. The jeep, purloined from an American contact I'd made locally, purred uncharacteristically down the long drive to the main road. The garage proprietor, OC Transport, first mechanic to Henry Seagrave pre-war, had applied unsuspected skills to the jeep's engine, transforming it into mechanical poetry.

The suspension, too, rode cushion-like with new shock absorbers, giving a touch of luxury to this crude contraption, as we sped 110 miles to a riotous, hectic twenty-four hours never to be forgotten.

2

DAWN IS RELUCTANT to appear. Leave is over. Our convoy of three vehicles arrives at Poole. Heavy rain and clouds darken the sky, sometimes reducing visibility to fifty yards. It's 6th August and news of the Hiroshima atomic bomb has just broken. Troops and civilians, aghast at the news, oblivious to the rain blowing in from the sea, stand around in disbelief, shocked by this unbelievable happening. Never been used in anger before!

Anxious to get to our destination and unsure, due to traffic diversions, which way to go, I brake at one of the groups and asked for RAF headquarters.

"On the dock, down by the jetty," was offered by a pretty young woman sergeant in the Women's Royal Air Force, whose smile sent messages to brighten this rain-soaked dull day.

"What do you think, Andrew?" asked May. "Will this bomb shut down the Jap war? I can't begin imagining the devastation and loss of life."

"It's a first, nobody knows," I say with thoughts elsewhere. My mind travelled back to Burma, 1942. Remnants of a beaten army retreated north on the only road to Mandalay; Japanese planes bombed the hell out of us, killing hundreds of brave Gurkhas—their bodies spattered into the roadside trees, unrecognisably dead. Atomic bombing of Japan would be more devastating, particularly to civilians, of whom there were millions.

"Don't know," was my reply, stifling emotion. "They might commit national hara-kiri or fight on more tenaciously. They're unpredictable little buggers."

❧

Out in the bay lay a Sunderland flying boat rising on the swell, lashed by driven rain and sea spray.

"That's your home for the next two days, at least," said the wing commander, long in RAF service, called back from retirement for his expert knowledge of flying boats.

Weather was putrid but Wingco was optimistic. "You'll be off inside one hour," he said with RAF certainty.

Weather improved, clouds broke up, and take-off was possible at exactly 1132 hours, I wrote in my journal. Wing Commander Bailey, about sixty, and tough as they come, waited to see our graceful ascent as the Sunderland became airborne, then, routine procedure, reported its safe departure to Movements HQ who, in turn, notified HQ 20th Indian Division in Burma.

❧

Once aloft, problems emerged. With a large party of thirty-two, kit and equipment had to be stowed so as to be readily available at the end of the journey.

Sergeant-Major Dawney, with many foul expletives, quickly formed a plan among other cargo already stowed haphazardly.

Finally, we settle down to rest as best we can for a three-day trip—maybe longer, with diversions, Wingco had told us. We discover to our pleasant surprise a keg of beer and large cans of fruit juice among the cargo. Our first loot and someone else's loss!

"We're now living rough. God help us if we go down with the squitters," remarked the sergeant-major, with his usual cunning smile. The latrine's a pair of thunderboxes; primitive washing facilities of a half-dozen bowls; unlimited quantities of coarse brown paper towels and tough, slippery bum paper. Shaving is discontinued for the duration of the journey.

I was thinking of Major-General Gracey somewhere to the north of Rangoon, at his 20th Indian Division HQ; he and his staff would be flat out selecting from his troops those most suitable for a military commission.

He knows I have his security and general intelligence in hand. What he must provide is men of special abilities in administration and public relations. He needs to find, from some 4,000 men and women, at least a dozen French speakers possessed of the social graces to take care of the many parties his HQ will have to provide for local dignitaries, and other PR purposes.

Flying at 20,000 feet the cabin becomes unpleasantly cold. With movement restricted between other cargo there's no chance to exercise. Engine noise discourages conversation beyond that absolutely essential; we confine ourselves to playing chess and card games requiring little or no talking—or merely resting.

Two days and a night before touchdown in Rangoon Harbour. We learn of the second atomic bomb, this time on Nagasaki. Relief at escaping from the confines of the plane is felt for no more than a moment as the impact of this appalling news sinks in. Two atomic bombs in three days is beyond belief.

"Why two bombs?" asked Carrysfort, addressing everybody. "Has someone flipped his lid in the White House? Surely one was enough to do the trick!"

"The Americans are telling the world—not just the Japanese," I explained, "that they are to call the tune from now on. Their message will be more for Russia and China, is my guess. Being the only atomic power, and likely to be so for years to come, they mean to condition other nations to their way of world control."

The route to 20th Division HQ was tortuous and crowded. Two hours to do twenty miles was nerve-fraying, and hard on one's patience. A few choice expletives found voice as we bullied our way through snarled traffic.

"Good to see you, Grant," welcomed the brigadier chief of staff, extending a hand. "How was your trip?"

"Bloody cramped, with thirty-two of us in a flying boat, sharing space with a pile of mail and cargo. Tell me, how does this second bomb on Japan affect our task?"

The dapper brigadier puffed at his pipe and admitted, "Haven't a clue," pushing back a wayward strand of black hair, a nervous gesture of disquiet over news of the atomic bombs.

I tried to picture the horror in the two cities—even shuddered a little as my thoughts visualised the scenes. "I suppose it's the only way the Japs will know they're beaten. Tough and terrible it may be, it's better than having this war drag on for—God knows how long."

"Sure," replied the brigadier, "if it works." He calmly polished the pipe bowl on his sleeve as he pressed the intercom lever. "Major Grant's here, sir. Are you free?"

As I entered the office Major-General Gracey came forward to greet me. There was mutual and indefinable accord from the minute we met in Matlook; this was confirmed as we now shook hands. The general agreed the atom bombs would now change things for Indo-China. Instead of fighting our way in, chances were the Japs would agree to a ceasefire. The British would still take over from the Japanese, remaining in control until a final decision came from Potsdam on how Indo-China would be governed.

Great excitement pervaded HQ. News had come that plans already made for the invasion of Malaya and eventual reoccupation of all enemy-held countries were being re-examined against the possibility of a Japanese surrender.

Speculation ended with General MacArthur's order forbidding reoccupation until he received the emperor's official surrender, timed for 2nd September.

My first port of call was to Lieutenant-Colonel Drury, a young, brilliant American OSS operative; pre-war an investigative journalist in Europe. Drury's presence had undertones: his relationship with Gracey had been soured earlier, in Burma, when he was refused Gracey's permission to fly the American pennant on his jeep.

I knew Drury well and liked him. He was, as most Yanks are, rough, even crude, but effective in Intelligence.

Drury was in the shower, singing some vulgar ditty at the top of his voice. During a lull in the musical entertainment I yelled, "How long you gonna be, Pete?"

For a moment silence reigned, then a Chicago voice thundered, "That you, Andy?"

"Yes!"

Stark-naked Drury leapt from the shower grabbing a towel and shook my hand vigorously, with real affection.

We'd worked closely together during the Jap occupation, operating spies, obtaining valuable information and infrequently having time to relax, enjoying one another's company. At times dispatching the odd nasty to his maker.

"I thought you'd be in this show, Andy, it is, after all, your home ground!"

"But why you?" I asked. "Thought you'd completed your assignment with my withdrawal last year. In fact, you had a row with Gracey; long time ago, I've forgotten where it was… something to do with flying a flag on your car, wasn't it?"

"I'm back for one very important reason. In our haste to get out, not get caught by the Japs, we'd no time to destroy those top-secret files—you remember them? Very embarrassing if they fall into French hands."

"I remember. You had them well hidden, as I recall. Don't you think they're still there?"

"Christ knows. I bloody well hope so. My orders are to find and destroy, or get lost."

"It's not like you to panic, Pete. If they're not in your hiding place, we'll sound out the village headman—he might help. Your old agents, too, should know. If they've gone, you've got a problem!"

"You're right," Drury surrendered. "I'll keep my cool. But I must insist on getting out on the first flight to Saigon."

"If you mean ahead of the general, I don't advise that," I warned. "Gracey's set his priorities for order of flight. Don't cross him on this, Pete. There's plenty of time after we land. You're number two in flight behind him. I'll go with you if you like, to check on the fate of the files."

"OK. By the way, how well d'ya know Gracey?" Pete asked, in a serious voice.

"Not well, I've only met him twice, at interviews. He seems good for the job we have to do. Why do you ask?"

"I've never liked him: we don't get on. He's got colonial mania, loves empires and white man's superiority. We've clashed many times over freedom for colonial peoples, notably in Syria, '41."

"He's not in a political role here. Our job is to disarm the Japs and confine them to barracks. We're in a holding role until a permanent administration is appointed."

"Take my word for it, Andy, Gracey will make it political. He'll have the French restored to power. He has no time for Ho Chi-minh and his dreams of independence!" This was said with force and a touch of anger, even ugliness.

I left Drury to meet up with Paul Hunter, my mind disturbed over the tirade I'd just received about Gracey. If the general *did* play politics I must be sure of my own position; I feared we may clash on matters of principle… must watch this general I'd hitherto thought neutral, after his dressing down by General Slim.

3

THE MORNING OF 11th September found number one military control commission poised for air-lifting to Saigon through Bangkok. Major-General Gracey arrived at the Rangoon strip and stood with his chief of staff checking details. It was just before first light when, from the far end of the runway, came the roar of exhausts and whining propellers. A DC 3, twin-engined transport plane, raced down the reserve grass runway and rose into the sky leaving fiery trails marking its ascent.

"For Christ's sake!" shouted the general. "Who the hell is that?"

"That's Drury's plane," answered the brigadier, timorously.

"The bastard!" swore the general. "Major Grant!" he yelled. "Ah, there you are. You know Drury, don't you?"

"Very well. Had a lot to do with him in guerrilla days."

"Why would he do this? I specifically told him to take off in order of flight, behind me. He agreed to this. So why?"

"Drury's under a lot of pressure from Washington. This doesn't surprise me. There'll be a good reason for it."

The general knew about the secret files, it had been pressure from OSS that persuaded him to allow Drury to join this mission. "It's those bloody files, I know. That's all he can think about... he made a cock-up not destroying them last time," shouted a very angry general. "I threw him out of my command before, and I'll do it again! As soon as you arrive in Saigon I want Drury found and brought to me," he ordered, making no disguise of his fury.

With a small team, I flew out ahead of the main party to ensure that the Japanese had complied with General Slim's orders about keeping the Vietcong guerrillas away from the airport and city of Saigon. Now I had another purpose— to find Colonel Drury and persuade him to see Gracey as soon as possible!

Our light RAF plane circles Saigon Airport waiting for clearance to land. The Japanese are busy doing usual things around the terminal building and alongside the runways, but there's no sign of guard troops. I assume they are positioned round the perimeter of the field. All appears peaceful and safe to land as Air Traffic Control orders us down. The Japanese behave skilfully, handling the plane into its parking bay, and impeccably in providing transport to my complete satisfaction. The Japanese airport commander assures our British party that Vietcong have been contained and prevented from entering Saigon. I ask about the arrival of Colonel Drury, whose plane has been parked under trees, not visible from the air. I am told Drury's party consists of twenty men.

In the city our group broke up: Sergeant-Major Dawney and others to previously assigned tasks, while I went alone to find Drury. Of the two cars provided by the Japanese, I took the Citroën sedan. I made for the northern outskirts of the city, where the Americans had a clandestine HQ used by undercover operatives of the OSS. I'd been there a couple of times and knew it to be a veritable store of valuable information, much of it highly sensitive and embarrassing to the USA if taken by the French. I felt certain Drury would have this as his prime objective.

Could just make out the place as, motoring slowly along the dusty road, I saw three vehicles: one car and two light trucks. My thoughts crystallised, I was right, Drury was here with his men.

Silence is shattered as a short burst of machine-gun fire rattles out, followed by another, then another, until it seems a small battle rages. I stop the car; men come running out of the building—some never to run again; they're dead before reaching the steps they rolled down into the unswept gutter. It was over in a flash. The Vietcong collected their dead and vanished taking the vehicles with them. That they had won this encounter was shockingly obvious.

I check to see my sten-gun is ready and primed, for unexpected surprises. Approaching cautiously; nothing moves in the village. Drawing nearer, I count fifteen bodies strewn over the steps and in the roadside, clad in the familiar tropical uniform worn by Americans.

I reach the building and leap from the car, looking into Drury's face and the gaping hole from which blood flows. As a matter of routine I kneel to feel if, by some odd chance, he has a pulse.

I become angry with Drury for not waiting till the place

is safe. I was fond of Drury, having been in many a tight corner together, and now I've lost a friend. His death will be mourned in Chicago where Drury's close relations live.

Without pausing to examine the others, I go quickly into the building. There I find five more bodies, making the total twenty—as told by the Japanese airport commander. I check and find none still breathing. I'm sickened by the sight, not because they are dead but of the wasted lives that need not have been.

Knowing the hiding place Drury used to conceal documents, in steel boxes under a heavy sideboard, I look to see if furniture has been moved and am surprised to find things apparently undisturbed. I wondered if this meant the documents were still there and my curiosity demanded closer examination. Only just in time did my sixth sense tell me to get out, as simultaneously my ear caught the familiar sound of a ticking clock. Turning rapidly, I ran, leaping over bodies, just managing to reach a monsoon drain large enough to dive into, as the building took off in all directions.

When noise of the explosion and falling debris ceased I climbed out of the drain to see the devastation, not only to this quite substantial place but to all the native wooden shops on either side—they too had vanished. A thin smile formed as I realised Drury had achieved his goal very bravely, like a damn fool! His secret files were, now, no more.

In view of the Japanese commander's assurances that the Vietcong had been kept out of Saigon, I thought it strange they had ventured this close to a village virtually on the edge of the city.

No point, now, in worrying about Drury and his men, they were beyond care except to see about their burial. I looked for and found the frightened village headman, who undertook this task in their local cemetery. I rewarded him suitably from Intelligence funds always carried on such occasions for a variety of purposes, and found a bag for the American name tags. I let the headman keep the wristwatches, having satisfied myself nothing else recoverable was on the bodies.

I recalled the many times I'd worked in clandestine operations with Drury and knew that a close working relationship had existed between him and the Vietcong guerrillas: so why had they now killed him? Something was wrong, I told myself, as I examined my car, removing rubble and splintered chunks of wood from its roof and bonnet. But what was wrong? This worried me, for it was out of character.

I got slowly into the Citroën, deep in thought and disturbed at this tragedy of killings. I turned the key, pressed the starter mechanically and drove slowly back to the city, to the other urgent task of dealing with the Kempei-Tai, Japanese military police. Their ruthless and powerful organisation contains members known to be war criminals of one variety or another, and I owe it to the many people of several nationalities that not one of these evil men escape the punishment they deserve.

Stopping the car at the Place Théâtre just south of the Continental Palace Hotel on Rue Catinat, the main shopping area—once graced by smart emporia, now grubby through neglect—I looked across the road to a tall building where upper-floor windows framed laughing, happy, French faces. Tricolours and—strangely—a Union Jack waved enthusiastically. A large shop occupied the ground floor, its windows displaying, surprisingly, an array of goods including many strings of Japanese cultured pearls. All nationalities of people on this side of the road stood either chatting, or sauntering from one group to another. Were they happy? No way of telling... there was no laughter here, just blank faces, while "Vive les Anglaise! Vive La France!" was shouted from the windows; I waved my thanks, with the familiar thumbs-up. This seemed to break the ice. Apprehensively, someone came to me and smiled shyly at this foreign-looking soldier. Then, more boldly came others to touch and shake my hand, saying "Merci, pour la liberation!"

Sergeant Ferris, a pre-war solicitor, now my specialist interrogator, stood talking to the unmistakable figure of Dr Eddie Blitz, PhD, one of my secret agents—a sallow-faced Jew of some thirty years and odd shape: his backside disproportionately large for his narrow shoulders, and a head absurdly small for the extremely thick neck supporting it. Ferris pointed to me, and Blitz waved as he turned down the avenue to Cholon, a suburb of Saigon in which Chinese merchants lived, where also Kempei-Tai headquarters occupied the handsome Chamber of Commerce building.

I am now surrounded by chattering crowds who join us in conversation. I'm trying to answer all their questions in a mixture of French and Cantonese. They ask: "What's to become of us?" "Who's in charge when you go away?" Fear of the future's unknown hung on their every word and smiling nervously gave way to women's tears.

Ferris crossed the road to report that Blitz had gone to the Chamber of Commerce building to tell Major Tomita, the Kempei-Tai commander he was to remain there with all his men. Ferris found it difficult to make himself heard as he, too, became the new centre of this surprise, spontaneous outpouring of bonhomie from friendly but frightened voices, seeking assurances of peace and happiness.

"I said you'd be there in about an hour. That OK?" he managed to shout into my ear.

"That's about it. When we've finished at the hotel and airport," I shouted back between handshakes from the mass of people now surrounding us.

With Ferris I managed to ease away, though some of the more inquisitive stayed in pursuit, determined not to lose us, as though we represented security against a return of colonialism.

At the main entrance to the hotel, a Japanese sentry sprang noisily to attention and presented arms as we moved up the few steps into the main hall, waving goodbye to the crowds. Obviously, the place was neglected throughout the years of occupation and now sadly and sorely needed renovation. Signs of its former glory could be seen in the graceful columns and grand staircase, but they were no longer white, dust and graffiti disfigured them. The treads, like the floor of the hall and passages, were tessellated with marble mosaics of many colours, now dulled with grime.

Sergeant-Major Dawney came out of a door to the right, wondering what the racket was all about. He flashed his most splendid salute on seeing me and reported that things were just as expected. "This place is full of very frightened French women, and a few Vietnamese who've managed to get away from gangs of unruly youths raping and pillaging. The report you received at the airport, sir, was dead right. Law and order has broken down, there's no police and the Japs have no civil authority."

A Japanese officer, flanked by two of my field security sergeants, emerged from a room on the right of the lobby.

"Colonel Hitaki," sneered Dawney. "He represents the local garrison commander. He's retained his HQ here because the Kempei-Tai have not been confined to barracks, as ordered by the Supreme Allied Commander."

I was not surprised by this, knowing the special powers of the Kempei-Tai. I wanted confirmation on rumours of threats and intimidation by Tomita's men against those who could testify to war crimes.

"Yes," confirmed Dawney, "this is so, the colonel has proof of it. This is why the HQ has been retained here so that those threatened can come for protection."

Speaking in Japanese, I told Hitaki to provide a nominal roll of the Kempei-Tai personnel in the Chamber of Commerce building. This he did instantly.

With Dawney I reached the airport to find Major-General Gracey's plane already landed with five others of the first flight coming in close to one another. I saw in the western sky twelve troop-carrying Dakotas approaching, looking like two flights of geese in formation. The airport was alive with action. The first wave of six Dakotas landed quickly with unloading well underway. Piles of bags and boxes stood by each plane as trucks were manoeuvred into position for loading by bare-chested Japanese soldiers, glistening with sweat.

Hunter, who had seen me arrive, reported both teams ready to move off to the city. I told him to report to the Palais de L'Indo-Chine for the time being. "I'll come to you later and we'll find you permanent homes for both sections."

The sun well up and humidity almost unbearable on this tropical September morning; no cooling breeze disturbed the listless fronds of the palm trees bringing relief to the perspiring freight handlers.

I spotted the chief of staff fussing in his usual way, trying to be everywhere at once, quite forgetting he had subordinates highly qualified to perform. Gracey was on the far side of the parking bays with a group of French officers and civilians.

No direct route to the general could be seen at first glance. I picked my way through and around piles of gear of all sorts, unloaded from the many aircraft carrying the commission's essential stores. Eventually I made towards him. On the way I exchanged banter with Lieutenant-Colonels Fugles and Cash, both first-class staff officers, who remarked good humouredly but inanely that "some people were lucky not having to work for their living." I reached the general as he was about to enter a shiny black limousine flying a Union Jack from the bonnet. I made a quick report about Drury and told him I was going to the Kempei-Tai HQ, at the Chamber of Commerce building in Cholon. "I want these evil bastards behind bars, pronto," I told the general, angrily, and departed in search of the provo marshal to arrange for a section of military police to report to me there.

I pulled up in front of the Chamber of Commerce, a large building with access through an enormous opening flanked by tall columns in Gothic style and a long flight of mosaic steps.

The lone sentry standing guard went through a formal routine of saluting us. A Japanese officer appeared at the top of the steps, leaving me with no doubt—he was the most important man at Kempei-Tai HQ. Legs slightly astride with both hands resting on the hilt of his Samurai sword, he made a picture of miniature might. His whole immaculate shortness bore that unmistakable mark of arrogance and cunning associated with Japanese military police. I noted the shining high boots, almost dazzling in the morning sun; a touch of the unusual in the two-tone pastel shades of the belt and matching sword knot; the imperious tilt to the head; and eyes that were slits bore a last stern, mock challenge to the approaching conqueror. Thus, Major Tomita, Kempei-Tai, commander, prepared for the inevitable, stood rigidly to attention; his face expressionlessly pale.

Undaunted, I mounted the steps with Sergeant-Major Dawney, correctly one pace behind, others to the rear. Tomita, moving slowly with unexpected grace, his sword in the left hand, hilt to the rear, clicked his heels together and bowed while saluting. This evil little Japanese policeman is determined that his surrender shall be immaculate to the last detail.

In such situations, I prefer to use a language other than the subject's native tongue: it sometimes gives an edge if he thinks you don't speak his language. I wondered about Tomita's knowledge of English and decided, after three years of interrogating French people, he must speak enough French.

Tomita drew in his breath as he straightened, still holding the salute, and said in flawless English of American origin, "Major Grant, I am at your disposal."

I stifled a grin at this choice of words. "Indeed you are," was my thought.

Tomita, about to speak again, was silenced by my moment of authority: "Parade all your men on the ground floor, immediately," I ordered. "I want a complete nominal roll of everybody on these premises, from the day you entered to now. You understand what I mean?" I was vehement in the tone of voice I employed.

"Yes, major," Tomita replied, handing over the millboard he had slung over one shoulder. "Everything you need is here."

Turning about he went quickly into the main hall and barked an order. It brought immediate results. Movement started above, boots clattered on stairways and passages, producing running men in all degrees of dress. Tomita barked again, suddenly it was perfect order, each man in his place forming four straight lines. Something seemed to concern Tomita; before he could act, or speak, the silence was shattered by a revolver shot coming from the top of the building.

First up the staircase, my mind was full of stories of Japanese committing suicide. As I reached the top floor, about to search the rooms, Tomita called from behind me: "It's on the roof!"

"Who is he?" I asked, looking down on the crumpled form

whose head oozed blood from a gaping hole in the temple.

"Sergeant Kito, a Korean," Tomita replied, showing no emotion.

"Is he the only one missing?" I demanded.

"Yes, major."

We returned to the ground floor to find the section of Military Police arrived, as ordered. I was pleased to see transport for carrying the Kempei-Tai to gaol. The nominal roll I gave to the officer in charge with instructions to prepare for interrogations to commence as soon as possible. "They're probably all war criminals of one kind or other, we have to grade them into categories—black, grey or white," I explained.

"The general told me to let you know, he'll be at the Palais de L'Indo-Chine," said the lieutenant.

Always hot on detail, I told him to compare the nominal roll with the one I'd brought from the hotel. "If you find discrepancies, get the truth from Tomita," I ordered. "And get these sods into gaol, soon as possible! God, the smell of them is worse than a nursery of slobbering babies sucking at their mothers' breasts... and search them now, for weapons!"

4

THE PALAIS DE L'Indo-Chine, former administrative HQ of French colonialism, is a large and handsome edifice. I installed myself in three rooms at the rear of the building. This location was selected as it had all the requirements for security; particularly a private entrance for visitors not wishing to be seen. It also put me close to the general.

I called in Hunter and May, and together we finalised the tactical siting of the two security sections. Looking at the town plan and the country areas, we saw at once that the original arrangement needed a wider spread than first thought. For maximum eyes-and-ears results a subsection was needed at Dalat, the popular hill station used by French ex-pats during the hottest weather from June to August. I could now get on with the important business of gathering information; assessing political and economic intentions.

The garrulous Eddie Blitz was in his office, back of an old school building on the ground floor—Eddie had a thing about it being much easier to leave a building in a hurry by the back door if you are on the ground floor! One of his sagacious sayings—of which he had many.

Blitz had been waiting, knowing I would contact him as soon as possible: he was my first in line, meaning he was always consulted early on, as a sounding board, about plans and intentions. Nobody working for me ever knew the whole plan, so it could never be revealed under torture.

Blitz smiled his welcome, I nodded in recognition. No familiar words were necessary; both knew our relationship was unchanged, despite my absence and the new conditions in Indo-China.

"Well," I began, "what's the score?"

Blitz went back to his chair behind the desk, and brought out his enormous and elaborately carved solid gold box—his "emergency money", heavy but portable. It doubled as cigarette container so was useful, too, he always said with a nervous chuckle, when showing it off to his friends.

"Have one," he invited, while forming a reply to the question. "Much has happened since you left and we now have a very confused situation. In general terms, Ho Chi-minh has us guessing. He's flirting with both China and Russia. He reckons on this worrying the Allies, thus preparing the ground for offers of co-operation with some form of independence."

I reflected: "Before leaving here in January he was doing some kind of deal with the Chinese, as I recall. Chiang Kai-shek was willing to become involved but, you will remember, we felt that Mao Tse-tung was in the background. Have you anything more on this?"

"Nothing hard, but there is good reason to believe Chiang and Mao have a deal of some kind. It has something to do with Mao's communists taking over in China and Chiang being found an alternative domicile—like Formosa. If Ho does do a deal with Chiang, and Mao takes over China, Ho's lost; for they will also take over Indo-China since they are connected by land. Obviously, Ho's best bet would be a deal with Russia for the very reason that they are geographically separated. A suitable treaty of this kind would protect Ho against Chinese ambitions and leave him free to pursue his policy of race purification, and," added Blitz sadly, "it's the ethnic Chinese who will suffer should that happen."

I reminded him that this paradox arose because the local Chinese had, over the years, dominated the business life of the country, rendering the Vietnamese second-class citizens in their own country—performing only the menial tasks in society.

"Ho will threaten to reverse these roles unless he gets his way, and you can imagine the pressures on the Allies from the liberals—the faint hearted—to accept his terms."

"God help us," Blitz said in despair. "They'll cleanse me, too."

"On the other hand," I reminded him, "enormous pressure will come from neighbouring countries, Siam and others near enough to be alarmed. A powerful communist influence so near to them will dismay Malaya, Philippines and, of course, Australia and New Zealand. At this stage it's impossible to see a solution that satisfies all parties. We must look for some alternative scheme."

Blitz had serious doubts for the future well-being of Indo-China based on his observations throughout the occupation. "The calm, pleasant life under France has gone, never to return, even if the French are allowed to carry on as colonialists. Everything has changed. Relations between ethnic groups are soured, it's now every man for himself; trust has vanished.

"Fraternisation with the Japs has resulted in some or all races being hated and targets for punishment such as ostracism; sometimes worse in cases of cohabitation.

"Don't forget, we have Marxist French already at work within this country. There's been scuffles at several meetings between opposing factions. Also, a youth organisation is gathering strength to defend their birthright; these are whites and some Eurasians born here. They're becoming very active and aggressive."

"As I thought, it's a fair mixture of problems. You've got this in writing for me?"

"Yes," said Blitz, opening a drawer and handing over a folder. "The most troublesome item in there concerns a policeman—Charles Aubaire. I'm afraid you may have to do something about him quickly. Maryse can tell you best but, as I understand it, Aubaire is preparing for her arrest on charges of cohabiting with the enemy. He's put it this way, I believe, because he's furious that she won't let him make love to her. He had 'collaborating' on the first charge sheet and changed it to 'cohabiting' to sound like sex with the Japs which, as you know, is worse for Maryse—a much more serious charge."

"Of course, we know he doesn't have a case, don't we, Eddie?" I replied. "What Aubaire doesn't know is that she acted under orders from me, for excellent reasons of intelligence. But, for equally good reasons, we can't tell him this without blowing her cover. Sex played no part in it, she was feeding the Japs false information. So, as you say, I may have to do something about him. Can't have one of ours blackmailed like this, can we!"

I gave him a folder with photos of Hunter and May.

"Other pictures and information will be fed as required, in the usual way. Anything more?" I turned to leave by the back door.

"No, that's it for now," Blitz replied, shaking my hand firmly to reinforce the bond between us.

I decided to reverse the order of contacts and see Maryse next, and Sie-ling later that night. Both, like Blitz, would be waiting for me to contact them, but with the telephone service not yet restored, word to Sie-ling would be sent by courier. This was a job for Peter Benoit, my special aide since Force 136 days. Benoit came into the office, as always the same lively exciting man, ever ready for action. I would use him more as things developed; it was necessary for him to meet Sie-ling now. I took a small box from a desk drawer and laid the contents out for Benoit to see.

"Here's the button which is your identity, and a photograph of Cheong Sie-ling. He must be at Club 46 by midnight. He knows where it is. Here's his address. Take my jeep—and don't be too long."

Born in Martinique, Benoit's French had a touch of the West Indies about it, but his Annamese was as that of a native, his teachers being the villagers with whom he lived for two years and the guerrillas he had fought with against the Japanese in the north of the country. He knew the language inside out; the coarse and the smooth. He passed for white, but only because his features were Caucasian. The powdered texture of skin, bequeathed by his beautiful octoroon mother, was acceptable as a result of years spent in the sun. He was, indeed, one of my remarkables.

I thought hard about Aubaire. The idea of him ravishing Maryse was repugnant. I knew Maryse intimately: never was there a more fastidious female over lovers. As with opium, which she used purely for mental stimulation, lovemaking was something very special to her. If Aubaire, chief superintendent of Sureté, known to be a communist sympathiser, insisted, trouble was sure to come.

I changed from uniform into cotton slacks and multi-coloured shirt. From the top drawer of the tallboy I took a flat wooden box and my favourite Belgian automatic. I slipped them into my back pockets, concealing them with the shirt worn loose outside my slacks. My watch told me time was just right to catch Maryse before she became involved at her intimate bar, playing host to her special customers.

Turning into Rue Colombier, I pulled up short of the club's main entrance. The night was still and hot; its sky aglow with starlight. A scene of many memories was this place; with its Spanish architecture and graceful columns enclosing a broad patio alive with boisterous humanity seeking the happiness so long denied them during the Japanese occupation. Each caring only for tonight—leaving tomorrow to its fate.

It was here I first met Maryse, two years back. While the night was much the same, the scene was very different. Then, Japanese officers and their local ladies occupied the patio; I'd hidden in the bushes while Sie-ling went in search of help for the wound that throbbed as the poison spread in my leg.

I sat in the jeep, feasting my eyes on the revelries, marking the awesome difference between the two moments. My hand moved to the lump on my thigh. It reminded me how near to death I'd come when the Vietcong's dart tore into my flesh that night. It was Sie-ling who had known where to find Dr Albert Simone, and Maryse who'd nursed me through delirium and fever.

As I relived those idyllic days of my close relationship with Maryse, the idea of Aubaire screwing her was abhorrent!

I jumped down from the jeep, taking in the scene, adjusting to the mood and preparing for a reunion with Maryse. A trickle of sweat released itself from my shirt. At the middle of my back, it tickled its way to my waist and was lost in the top of my slacks. August tropic nights can be sticky and this one was proving the point. Coconut palms and palmettos hung still in the humid dusk; even the dance music filtering from the club clung to the dank, dark air, a little stifled. I confessed to a feeling of desire for Maryse, once my constant companion.

A steady stream of fun seekers moved down a path bordered on both sides by lovely double yellow hibiscus; voices suggested more a continuation rather than a beginning to their jollity. "Vive les Anglaise," shouted a big-breasted blonde in voice slightly slurred, to no one in particular. I thought this the right moment to mingle with the crowd and enter the club inconspicuously. I was soon among the happy, noisy bunch of youngsters.

At the steps leading up to the patio I found myself alone,

the others melting into the scene. It had been a long time since youth's infectiousness had stirred that something inside me; I was pondering this when from behind I heard, "Bienvenue, major."

This aristocratic voice I knew so well. Turning, I found beside me glamour and desirability in female form: her hair shone like gleaming copper in the artificial light; the eyes were alive with green flashing darts as she moved to the music's rhythm; the mouth could be nothing but sensuous—lips full, moist and slightly apart. Her dress, cunningly designed to excite, clung to a body of stunning desire. The slit from the waist, cleverly made to look like a pleat, revealed shapely legs as she came closer to me. Youth's infectious spirit, I was thinking, had put a keener edge to my sensibilities. At thirty, this was hard to accept; I concluded, the lady had to take all the credit.

"Maryse, chérie, je suis arrivé plus vite."

Always there had been mystique about this ravishing female member of one of France's hundred first families. Her dossier read like a bestseller. This beautiful, gifted aristocrat ran away from parental restraint on her eighteenth birthday and fetched up in Saigon. She had survived and succeeded in a colonial society to whom the kind of things she did were both outrageous and unladylike.

Her greeting had much meaning, and I found myself with thoughts other than those of work. The vision had been created deliberately and cleverly. Sheer basic lust dominated for a while. I even toyed with the more devious aspects of desire. I seduced her mentally—as she did me.

A slight welcome breeze wafted over us disturbing her hair, pressing the thin dress against her thighs and belly, revealing to my experienced eye her underneath nakedness. The effort of self-denial brought beads of sweat to my face and rivulets cascading down my back.

Suddenly I felt calmer and in control. She had missed nothing, her smile said everything. "Vien," she invited, turning to lead me, as I thought, to her bedroom.

She moved between hibiscus shrubs, over an ornamental pond with its bamboo bridge and miniature pagoda. She was ahead of me, I closed the gap as she turned the eastern corner of the building. Now on a flagged walkway that circled the building, leading to the rear without being seen from inside the club. She unlocked a door and flipped a switch.

I found myself in another world, full of mystery: the air charged with the sweet aromatic smell of opium; the lighting strangely dim; shapes shone dully—a dark carmine reflected rich red from a small oil lamp in the centre of the room. All was new to me, though I was sure I'd been in this room many times. It was the lighting and changed layout that disorientated me.

Maryse took my hand but said nothing as she guided me towards the lamp. The walls, draped with dragons embroidered on fine tapestries, and the furniture I could just make out, were exquisite and oriental. I felt baffled by the lighting—obviously some indirect system, but how was it done?

"How the hell do you light this place?"

Knowing exactly how to handle men, even when on strictly official business, she replied, "Come, I'll show you."

The centrepiece revealed itself as a circular divan richly

covered in crimson brocade, the oil lamp in its bright red chimney resting on an ivory column in the centre.

"To see its cunning, you must lie on your back and look up... reposé toi, chéri," Maryse invited tenderly.

I lay back and she lay beside me. "Regard," she softly explained, pointing to the ceiling, "those reflectors receive jets of light, so fine the eye cannot see, and diffuse them to a barrage of spun glass strands. These in turn transmit the light to coloured discs of magnifying glass angled out of the line of sight. Japanese genius at its best, n'est ce pas?"

Before I could reply, she was astride me, pinning my arms to the silken divan. Her mouth found mine, while her body moved against me, pressing down hard to meet my upward thrust. When at last my hands were free to roam, she was naked. She nibbled my ear and whispered, "Now."

❧

We lay exhausted, physically satisfied. We both knew, somehow, that to make a session of it would spoil things. Just once, so perfect after so long, should, like a flawless gem, remain solitary.

Planting a kiss on my mouth, she sprang from the divan trailing her flimsy dress in one hand.

"Un moment, darling," she said, and was gone, so calmly, as if leaving her office for something or other.

❧

I was fascinated by this complete change from the amorous to the matter of fact in a flash. Kittenish one moment and coolly mature the next. She had, of course, done it before, but this time was different; she was radiant, like someone in love. I awaited the next scene with more than ordinary interest. Meanwhile, I took a closer look at the room. Not as large as I remembered it. The reason, I discovered on getting up from the settee, was that an alcove had been formed at one end.

I moved the bead curtain aside to reveal a familiar scene. The opium smoker's oil lamp was housed within a narrow necked green glass chimney. On a tray of beautifully worked copper it stood, surrounded by smaller trays, dishes and long-stemmed pipes with unusual bowls, each with a central hole to receive the needle of opium. One tray in particular caught my eye, for, unlike its companions, it was not decorated with semi-precious stones. Its attraction was in the array of what appeared to be tools: plain steel thin rods; a penknife; scissors; other things that looked like scrapers. All this was placed in the centre of a wide, board-like bed covered with straw matting. In here the smell of opium was strongest. I knew this had to be her new opium chamber—as Maryse preferred to call it. Though not a smoker myself, I had often lain with her and wondered at her ability to control it and not become an addict. She obviously had need of it.

I was thinking what a rare breed she was, when I heard: "Interested in opium now, darling?"

She had arrived without a sound. I had not even sensed her being there, so deep in thought had I been. I was thinking nobody would ever guess that we were making passionate love only a few moments ago.

"One day," she said, "when the time is right, you shall try it with me. You'll love it. But now we must talk, chéri. First, a drink to your return."

A small bell of engraved gold colour tinkled lightly in her long tapering fingers, and almost immediately a silent servant stood beside her. Slight and exquisitely beautiful, her black hair piled high and wide, shining like polished ebony, in contrast to the beautifully carved ivory combs holding it in place. The dress was long, high at the neck, split on both sides to the hips. Beneath, as she moved, peeped flimsy silks of different shades in perfect harmony. Her dainty feet were bare.

Maryse spoke softly, as to a child, in Annamese. The girl, her arms crossed in front, bowed slightly and came to me.

"May I prepare the honourable major some refreshment?" she asked in flawless French. Maryse smiled, watching my reaction.

"Merci," I replied, fascinated by the sheer beauty of her. "Whisky avec la glace, s'il vous plâit."

Maryse told her—crème de menthe frappé—her usual social drink, and we relaxed in fan-shaped bamboo chairs.

I sensed she was on edge so waited for the lovely little Annamite to leave the room, then said, "Eddie Blitz tells me Aubaire of Sureté is making a bloody nuisance of himself. If there's no way of buying him off, I'll have to remove him."

"There's only one way, and I'm not willing to pay his price. You know me, chéri, I'm fussy about men," Maryse said in anger. "I had in mind arranging an accident, but I need help."

The beautiful one returned, placed a tray with fine china bowls of tasty things and our drinks on the lacquered table between us and was gone, bowing silently.

I took the flat box from my pocket and opened it. "You remember this, don't you?"

Maryse nodded, she had used the contents before. She relaxed and smiled. "What would I do without you, Andrew darling?"

I smiled, too. I knew that she was quite capable of dealing with Aubaire, her dossier proved that. "You just need me to make it look like an accident," I teased.

"Darling, he's due here tonight," she began, in mock fear, "to *have* me or *arrest* me! You don't want either to happen, do you? Besides, he's a villain who has to be dealt with because of his political activities."

"OK—I'll arrange it. Now, tell me what the general situation is in the country."

I knew, in Maryse, was a very special agent – a very special woman, too. She confirmed what Eddie Blitz said and gave me three names of particular importance: Professor Lien, a Chinese communist, a newcomer of whom I had already heard; Nuyen Van Hua, Ho Chi-minh's man, already known from occupation days; lastly, Boris Ulowski, Russian, another newcomer. Maryse felt these were the men to watch. She also confessed to being puzzled over the activities of a youth movement in which Marie-Claire Simone was very active.

On the other side was Chiang Kai-shek's Major Lim Ten-moi who described himself as an observer. Maryse thought him more a two-faced bastard set on making political capital.

I told her about Hunter and May, and left a file with photographs for her to learn and destroy.

5

RUNNING UP THE stairs to an apartment I used for covert purposes, neatly situated above a café, I puzzled over the activities of Marie-Claire Simone. What was the daughter of my old doctor friend doing in a fanatical youth movement—something akin to political dynamite! Maryse confirmed that she was certain of Marie-Claire's prominent role in the movement's affairs. I wondered if the doctor knew about this, if he approved or, perhaps, had no option or control over his daughter.

A tap on the door was distinctive, in four short and two long pauses, just as expected. It was the signal of my special agent Cheong Sie-ling, Cantonese by ethnic origin, born twenty-eight years ago in Cholon to rich merchant parents. In student days—in Paris and London—politics so fascinated him he switched from business to political studies. To placate his disappointed father, whose ambition was for his brilliant son to succeed him and expand the family business, Sie-ling agreed to read economics and law as well.

A small man of nondescript appearance, the dominant feature a smile—subtle and disconcerting. Sometimes, he wore it to deceive; at others, in genuine pleasure. Only his intimates knew the difference. For me, it beamed real affection as he entered the apartment. He was, indeed, a "slipper"; moving noiselessly. Sie-ling clasped my hand with his two hands, a special gesture of close friendship and loyalty.

"Good to have you back, Andrew," was his warm and sincere greeting.

We talk for an hour. Sie-ling explains the situation, confirming what Blitz and Maryse had said, adding extra details about a secret Chinese organisation formed to counter communist propaganda.

"One final point," I said. "Assuming the Cholon Chinese accept that the French cannot return as colonialists, what arrangements are they working at?"

"They'll accept anything that ensures a continuance of their way of life. Obviously, the Russians are not wanted. Preferably, they want a democratic system of the capitalist variety."

"Do they talk of partition?"

"This is really what they want if colonialism is dead."

"I take it they're prepared to oppose any arrangement contrary to their liking?"

"They'll use every trick, violent or otherwise."

"Taking the long-term view, say partition comes and fails and Chinese or Russian communism becomes the order of the day, what are they likely to do?"

"Those who could would leave the country. The rich without much difficulty; they have assets abroad. The rest as best they can by any means at any risk. If they leave it too late, the sea will be the only way out, using anything that will float!"

I closed the door behind the slight figure who said softly, "See you later."

We both had crucial roles to play in the dispatch of a policeman, Superintendent Aubaire.

It was 2330 hours, I wanted to round off the first day with Hunter and May, updating myself with the general situation. I wanted also a hand with Aubaire.

I pulled up at Hunter's HQ, a large house beside the cathedral on the top of the hill at the end of Rue Catinat. In two minutes we were off to May on the other side of town, in Dockland. In this case the house was not a pretty sight from the outside. May had found it occupied by a Japanese naval captain, Dock Master, whose taste in furniture and works of art was superb. May had kicked him out and taken over the property. Such was the power of a field security captain with the approval of his superior officer.

I dealt with the business of out-station communications first as Japanese troops were still in situ. "As soon as possible, move the out-station men into position," I ordered. "I want radio contact with the main stations by D plus two at the latest. The minor ones, like Dalat, can be even two days later." Much remained to be done, I must make time to prepare a report for the general and political adviser.

I was meticulous as to the best procedure in the matter of Aubaire. The business of dealing with troublesome people is almost routine in war conditions, when few official questions are asked. In peacetime it becomes more problematic, especially when the person is a senior police officer of an Allied country. For these reasons I had devised a simple and effective method of disposal, specially for post-war situations.

Sie-ling would know how to arrange for witnesses to a fatal happening. All that remained was the detail and from my considerable store of ideas in such circumstances, I had begun to finalise the most plausible cause of death.

Charles Aubaire, a policeman with a reputation for helping those who helped him, had a way of interpreting the opium laws regulating dens and those who used them, which was both novel and rewarding. Shady operations could function for a consideration. Stories were told of extortion and blackmail, Aubaire always connected in one way or other.

Maryse had cunningly acquired an old OSS file of political suspects; Aubaire's name was there. He took leave in Hanoi before the war; there he was seen in suspicious company by Saigon businessmen. Over a drink in the club, one of them mentioned it to the French military commander and surveillance began. In this file, a Chinese Professor Lien's name first appeared as one of Aubaire's contacts in Hanoi. I figured that, if the Americans knew about Aubaire's pre-war communist affiliation, the French would be under a cloud for not taking action against him before the war. Maybe they were unable to find evidence to hold up in law; no doubt Aubaire could argue he was acting officially. Maybe, I thought, the French would not mind if someone else removed him from the scene. Aubaire's partiality for coloured women gave me the setting required for this job of extermination.

Stafford May studied the file and smiled. "Who do you want to help in removing him?" he asked.

I responded, without hesitation, "I'll take Sergeant-Major Dawney with me. When Sie-ling comes, tell him to be at Club 46 by 2400 hours. He is to provide an address in the native quarter where special native ladies—not common whores—are available. I need willing and reliable witnesses to an accident. He'll know what I mean."

Aubaire arrives at Club 46, it's midnight; inwardly excited at the prospect of getting his way with Maryse, he'd fortified himself—with the usual result... his face is flushed from the effects of liquor. As normal, he assumes an arrogance intended to intimidate, to make up for shortness of stature. Maryse is at her usual place behind the small intimate bar in the corner—to which Aubaire moves.

A full house, both military and civilian in high spirits makes the atmosphere at once salacious, stinking hot and smoke-laden. Noisy chatter is growing louder by the second while drunken singing is doing its best to be heard against an increasing volume of raucous laughter.

Such had become the mood of the moment in this new-found freedom: anything goes, no restraint.

No other formula was acceptable; life must be lived to the full became the accepted rule.

Aubaire roughly elbowed his way through the merrymakers and arrived bad-tempered beside a young Foreign Legionnaire with ideas of his own about Maryse. Trying vainly to shoot a line, others at the bar poked fun at him; he swore at them, creating a dangerous disturbance.

"Enough of that!" ordered Aubaire with stern authority. This, and his senior police officer's uniform, proved too much for the youth, who decided it best to move on.

Aubaire watched Maryse at the other end of the bar, hoping for recognition of the masterly way he had dealt with the rude lout. Maryse, knowing she had time to spare, ignored him. Aubaire was sullen and hurt. He glowered hard at her, his face reddening a shade deeper. Suddenly, he demanded attention and ordered "Anise!" at the top of his voice. Everybody nearby went quiet and Maryse decided it best to serve him before trouble started. She poured the drink, then asked a young woman customer to pass it to the superintendent. Aubaire, inwardly furious, accepted the glass ungraciously. The woman looked at Maryse who nodded a signal to remain with Aubaire.

I showed myself briefly at the doorway, long enough to catch Maryse's eye who, taking her cue, moved to Aubaire saying, "Good evening, superintendent."

Aubaire took a moment before mellowing, then asked in his official voice, "Can I have a word in private with you?"

"Yes. One moment, while I get someone to take over here." She pressed a bell under the counter and poured more anise into his glass. "On me," she said coyly.

A young Annamite, whom Maryse had adopted as a small boy, lifted the bar flap and she slipped through, eager to get this over with.

"Come," she invited. Aubaire threw back his drink and followed her, in happier mood, if slightly more tipsy.

On the way to Maryse's private quarters, he was excited.

"Well?" he began eagerly, his voice slurred. "What's it to be?"

In her bedroom she put her arms around his neck. Kissing him, she asked, "Does that answer you?" while undoing his tunic.

Sergeant-Major Dawney and I had by this time reached the rear of the building where Cheong Sie-ling waited, having taken up a position providing direct vision into Maryse's bedroom.

We watch the scene unfold with Aubaire clumsily attempting to force Maryse to the bed, and her pretending to tease by running away.

It was when Aubaire caught up with her, grabbing her arm, that it happened: Maryse crushed herself against him; at the same moment, using her free hand, pressed a tiny plunger into his fleshy neck, piercing the jugular.

Aubaire felt the prick but nothing more as he collapsed heavily to the floor—dead from snake-venom poisoning.

Quickly, I and others removed the body and at speed made for the village chosen by Sie-ling, where arrangements had been made by Madame of the brothel frequented by Aubaire.

The scene was set, complete with the krait from which the venom was extracted whose fangs precisely matched the two holes made by the plunger Maryse used.

Of course, the snake is dead. Madame would tell the police how the brave girl with Aubaire had killed it.

I'm satisfied the plan is foolproof, providing everyone likely to be questioned by the police knows what to say. Leaving Sie-ling to deal with the final details I returned with Sergeant-Major Dawney to my office.

Maryse, unruffled, returned to her bar. She told her guests the superintendent made routine enquiries about things of little or no importance, of which she had no knowledge.

Looking at her watch and speaking the time, the hour of Aubaire's departure was established.

6

I ENTERED THE general's office to find a stranger there.

"Hello," he said, "I'm Peter Bain, political adviser. The general will be with us in a minute."

Bain was shorter than me and slight of frame. A typical government officer to look at; very neat in tropical suit and yellow bow tie. Black hair, flecked with grey and brushed flat above an open florid face of pleasing features. A kindly countenance, I thought, rather like my old games master at school. The eyes matched his hair, very dark and dominant beneath a full high brow. No fool, this one. Maybe not so typical, after all.

"I'm Grant, Special Operations."

"You've had a busy time, I hear," said Bain. "Sad about Colonel Drury, isn't it? You'll be telling us, when the general returns, why he took off like that. I'll be patient till then."

The general came through the door in jolly mood, he was humming *Le Marseillaise*! "Ah, good. You're both here. No need for introductions." Taking his place behind the sumptuous desk formerly used by French colonial governors, he invited us to sit.

I made my report with supplementary information on points of detail. Peter Bain was particularly disturbed to hear my opinion that the basic problem was Sino-Russian.

"This will dominate history from now on," I stressed. "No matter what arrangement is made, partition or anything else, it can only be a matter of time before one or the other takes control. Local Chinese fear that Russia will finally back Ho. They feel this will be bad for them. I have doubts about Russian influence, I'm certain China will go to bed with Ho Chi-minh."

"There's little doubt," said Bain, "the majority official view among Allied governments is for partition. The French, however, have suggested restoring Emperor Bao Dai over the whole country."

"The Americans support this, I understand," said the general.

"America argues that this is essential to gain time," added Bain.

"And at the end of time," I asked, "will they pretend Ho Chi-minh isn't there?"

"No one's got that far, I'm afraid," Bain replied. "At least, if they have, the Yanks aren't saying so."

"I don't believe partition will come until it has to," I said with emphasis. "My information is that de Gaulle will press for the whole country, including Cambodia and Laos, to become part of the French Union. If they succeed, it will be a tragedy and must lead to war. Ho would never accept it. He'll go on fighting from the jungle and, backed by Russia and/or China, must win in the end."

The general shifted in his chair fixing his eyes firmly on me, but said nothing. I had a good idea what was going through his mind. He dearly wanted the French to return as colonial master.

"About Drury," the general digressed. "You don't seem satisfied as to why the Vietcong killed him. I, too, am mystified when you tell us of the good relations he had with the guerrillas. Have you no ideas in your fertile brain about this, Andrew?"

"Not yet, sir. But, since the killing bore all the signs of a slick and well organised operation, I suspect a betrayal of some sort."

"That all? Or, all you're prepared to say at this time?"

"I've a few ideas, sir," I replied, allowing a faint smile to form.

"All right," said the general, adding firmly, "but, when *you* know, *I* want to know—understand?"

Tonight was to be one of rare quality in my business, giving me a golden opportunity to even things up with one Colonel Lucius Shaw of American OSS.

Colonel Lucius J Shaw II acquired a nickname from the moment he crawled under a bungalow in Bangkok and, with only one round in his service revolver, shot and killed a snake. From then on he was known as Colonel "One-Shot" Shaw.

Some use it in fun, even in the intimate sense in friendship. Others, who have no time for the man, call him "One-Shot" derisively. I hear it this way when joining a social group at Dr Simone's house.

Overhead turns a large ceiling fan, slowly, but enough

to disturb the clinging, hot, humid air. The motor hums loudly enough for conversation to be raised to counter the opposition.

Silence falls on the gathering at the insistence of a young American captain, who, for reasons untold, decides to introduce the newly arrived OSS colonel.

"Mesdames et messieurs, je vous present le Colonel 'One-Shot' Shaw," is said through thick lips in a voice more than slightly affected by liquor—and an edge of malice.

French women question one another, and one boldly asks the colonel if "One-Shot" is a first name or part of the surname. Obviously annoyed, Shaw glares at the captain, then cleverly turns the incident to his advantage. He tells the story from which the nickname was born, and all are amused.

"So you see," he drawled, "those not as deadly with the revolver like to pull my leg about it. That so, captain?" was tart and menacing.

I'd come to the party especially to meet Colonel Shaw, whose arrival from Bangkok was reported to me by Hunter's airport watchers. I had a purpose, was short of time, and wanted to make contact as soon as possible. A date had been made with the colonel for tomorrow morning but I decided his office was not the best setting for my purpose; besides, I wanted to combine this meeting with a special visit to the prison.

There's something sinister about senior OSS officers. Unmistakably, it borders on arrogance. Their training instils confidence of the highest order in those possessing the mental and physical qualities for the job. With competition for the higher posts intense, it's natural for the successful to feel superior.

Like me, Colonel Shaw belonged to the elite of the military machine. Counter Intelligence in the battlefield ascends to lofty planes; its operators enjoy special powers and freedom of action, particularly when feeding battle-winning information to combat generals. Similarly, those in the more sinister aspects of Intelligence, the covert branches, have wide powers in countering those of evil intent.

Colonel Shaw both looked and acted the part: he was superior; expert, too, in Far Eastern affairs; and ruthless. Although we had never met, each knew the other by reputation. Each had a file on the other.

Shaw stood about five feet ten inches with width of shoulder belonging to a weight lifter. Touches of grey at the temples added a few years to his forty. His dark eyes danced with vitality as he took in the room and its occupants. His mouth opened wider as he strained to hear what I was saying over lively chatter.

"Major Grant, you said? Oh yeah. I have you on my list for tomorrow. 1000 hours, isn't it?"

"Sure."

We moved away from the group at my suggestion. I led the American to the ante-room off the lounge while, in our place, came Madame Simone, the tall and beautiful young Eurasian wife of our host Dr Simone.

Formerly based in Bangkok, Colonel Shaw co-ordinated USA OSS activities east of India; it was almost certain that he would have been the link between Colonel Drury and Washington. He would therefore have known the reason behind Drury's impromptu departure from Rangoon's airport. This was the way my mind was working when word came earlier from Dr Simone that Shaw would be at the party. The doctor, a very important part of my scheme of things ever since the time he removed the poisoned dart from my leg, was as well informed as any operative. Through his medical practice the flow of information was continuous, as informers could come and go to his surgery without suspicion, reporting in the privacy of the consulting room. It was through a "patient" that the doctor learned of Drury's "meeting" with Major Tomita of Kempei-Tai.

"I'm going to the prison after this!" I announced to Colonel Shaw. "I wondered if you'd like to join me?"

"God! That's a rum place for two handsome guys to visit at this time of night," Shaw replied with questioning eyes. "I had in mind a nightcap at Club 46."

"We can do both. I'd like you to meet Tomita, the Kempei-Tai commander. I think you'll be interested in his answers to some questions I'm going to ask."

I knew the American sensed that he was about to be put on the spot. My reputation left no doubt that this invitation had a purpose. In fact, my being here at the party had a purpose; he'd be left with no option but to go along with my suggestion.

"Sounds interesting. Sure thing, major. I'd like to meet this sonofabitch. Heard bad things about him. Is he nasty, as they say?"

"First-class bastard," I affirmed. "He's for the chop—at the top of my war-criminal blacklist."

Marie-Claire, the doctor's daughter, interrupted us, offering canapés, which she described as delicious. Both of us were visibly affected by her sheer beauty. She had her mother's big dark green eyes, like pools of jade glinting and flashing as she smiled at me.

"Hello, Marie-Claire. Have you met Colonel Shaw?"

"Hello, major." She replied with a flick of the head, throwing a wayward lock of her jet-black hair into place. The lovely eyes lost some of their gleam and the smile vanished as she turned to Shaw. Instinctively she disliked him simply because he was American. She'd heard that America favoured giving token independence to Ho Chi-minh, and she said so.

"Where d'you hear that?" asked Shaw, concerned at her remark. "On the contrary, our official position hasn't yet been established. It can't be until a decision comes out of current discussions at Potsdam."

"Father Bouvier told us at mass this morning," she explained forcibly... as if the priest were incapable of being wrong.

"Wonder where he got it?" said a concerned Shaw. "I hope this isn't a widespread rumour. Could do a lot of harm."

Maryse's reference to Marie-Claire and the Youth Movement came to mind. I'd given it no great importance at the time, but somehow this boldness with Shaw on first meeting put another complexion on it. Marie-Claire had spoken in anger.

"You feel very strongly about this," I felt her out. "It affects your future, I can see."

"You bet I feel strongly about it. So do all of us who were born here. This is our home," was said hysterically. "You have eyes to see that I'm coloured, so is maman. We belong here, and the communists intend to eliminate us if they get independence, because we're of mixed race."

Much impressed by this outburst, I watched her heaving breasts as she regained her calm. How lovely she is, I thought, and how strong and wild. She was afraid and angry. But how far would she go, I wondered?

Venturing to mollify, I said, "Will you take it from me, Marie-Claire, that up to this moment no one on the official side has any intention of giving independence to Ho? And, even if later it is decided desirable to partition, there will be rigid safeguards for all the people."

"There you are," she snapped, "you admit to the possibility of something later. Call it what you will, partition is just the thin end of the wedge."

Her words had their effect on the others, who silently wondered about their own futures. Dr Simone reached her side, putting an arm around her to comfort her, saying in French, "Don't be afraid, ma petite, everything's going to be fine."

Hungry for reassurance, words like this brought relief to the tense atmosphere. Hope, mingling with wishfulness, brought "Vive de Gaulle" from one, followed by "Vive la France" from another.

"Vive les Anglaise," said a now laughing Marie-Claire, linking arms with me and kissing me on the mouth.

Small talk was abandoned as the mood, matching the moment, became once more subdued and serious. Shaw agreed with me that this was the time to leave the French to debate their fate, uninhibited. He told his driver to follow and got into my jeep.

Shaw had good reason to be apprehensive. The name Major Tomita as spoken by me worried him. My file on Shaw, among other revelations, contained the following report:

Before the war, in 1936, Shaw was young, at twenty-seven, in the United States Intelligence Service, learning the job.

Assigned to a team studying the behaviour of Japanese college students, he was drawn to suspicious activities of Yoshiro Tomita, an artist and photographer.

Tomita, being a skilled spy and aware of Shaw's immature attentions, played the oldest card in the pack, sex, thereby disarming Shaw. Being wealthy, he found it easy to befriend Shaw and throw him off the scent. Tomita gave lavish parties, with showgirls providing female delights, to which Shaw was always invited.

At the propitious moment Tomita disappeared with his sketches and photographs of highly sensitive subjects, leaving Shaw to find suitable excuses, with "mud on his face".

Shaw was staggered to find Yoshiro Tomita here in Saigon, and commander of the infamous Kempei-Tai.

The prison stood stark and ugly in silhouette against a strangely lit sky—giant concrete mass of four storeys surrounded by a very high wall. With a little imagination, it resembled a great liner with square portholes.

The French army, having taken over from the British, gave their toughest unit the job of running the prison.

Visitors found themselves confronted by a Foreign Legion sergeant whose devotion to duty as gate commander amounted to a searching identity enquiry. Satisfied of our bonafides, he asked the nature of our business. I told him we wished to see Major Tomita.

I had access to the Kempei-Tai prisoners but this sergeant, not authorised to allow visitors not on his list, had to phone the prison commander. After a few minutes we were cleared for the visit. A soldier was detailed to escort us to the third floor, where a corporal in charge of the landing took over.

He led us along a wide verandah open on one side to the extensive compound between blocks. On the other side were heavily barred cages, each housing up to twenty Japanese prisoners. At the end was a cage with only four occupants, one squatting apart from the others.

"He's in there," said the corporal, pointing.

I went to the bars and peered into the poorly lit interior. Tomita was the lone one.

"Come here, major," I ordered in Japanese.

The small figure rose from the squatting position and instinctively obeyed. His fine shiny boots had gone. He stood rigidly to attention, in his socks. The lacing of his breeches was undone as was the tunic, producing an image of despair.

I told Tomita I wanted accurate and complete answers to my questions. "I shall speak in English, and you will reply in English!" I explained this to Shaw, who had moved up beside me, telling him, "These questions are designed to extract vital information about your predecessor—Colonel Drury. I am hoping this may help us to understand the rash behaviour that led to his death."

"But," queried Shaw, "what would this Japanese know about Colonel Drury?"

"We'll find out." Turning to Tomita, whose face revealed nothing, I spoke with force. "I know that you were at the airport when Colonel Drury arrived. I also know you met him and gave him something." I paused, my gaze penetrating the mask and detecting the faintest twitch of a muscle beside Tomita's nose. "What did you give him?" I demanded.

There was silence as Tomita, his head cast down to avoid my eyes, weighed his position. The question had shaken him, but it had also revealed that I knew his terrible secret. He was afraid but decided not to counter by assuming his old arrogance.

"I gave him a file," he said calmly.

"About what?" I demanded.

After a long pause, Tomita hesitantly admitted, "It was my complete account of the Vietcong with personalities, military and civilian, together with their organisation, aims, objectives and strategy. I also included our appreciation of their strengths and weaknesses."

I noted the expression on Shaw's face change. Tomita appeared to be silently pleading for his help; or was it merely a pathetic surrender admitting defeat, saying "I have to tell all now"?

"Why did you give him this file?" I demanded.

Tomita's eyes betrayed him. He half-looked at Shaw, it seemed for help, then replied, "It was a deal." Still he looked at Shaw, questioningly. I thought there was a slight movement of Shaw's head. "I can't say," Tomita finally added, casting his eyes to the floor.

"Then I'll tell you what the deal was," I said slowly to

Tomita, while letting my gaze fall upon Shaw. "He promised to use his influence to minimise war-crimes charges against you in exchange for information. That was the deal, wasn't it? He'd promised you, hadn't he?" I looked back at Tomita. "And you believed him, didn't you? Answer me!"

"Yes," was the soft reply of surrender, more like an exasperated exhalation he could no longer hold back.

"Yes!" I almost shouted. "Then why did you tip off the Vietcong guerrillas and have him killed?"

Tomita stared hard at me, disbelieving his ears. How could I know so much? Tomita was unprepared for this. His meeting with Drury had been secret with no prying eyes. How had I found out? Only the Vietcong knew—so how?

"Well?" I asked impatiently.

"He betrayed me," growled Tomita. "As soon as he had the file he told me Washington would not agree to the deal."

"He deceived you, my friend. There's a subtle difference between betray and deceive." I transferred my gaze to Shaw, who was trying hard to conceal his true reaction to this.

ॐ

Nothing was said between me and Shaw as we left Tomita and the prison. It was not until I'd swung myself into the jeep that I said quietly, almost as an aside, "So now you know the score."

"Yeah, but I don't understand some of it," Shaw was doing his best to appear unaffected. But I knew that he must be very disturbed.

"Does it help you to understand when I tell you I've had you watched since your arrival in Saigon? I know you visited Tomita at his headquarters. My guess is you wanted a copy of the report he gave to Colonel Drury. You were unlucky. Tomita destroyed it along with all other incriminating evidence before we got to him. You blocked the deal. You never put the proposal to Washington. You lied, when saying they'd turned it down. Drury held on to the report that died with him. All you cared about was getting your hands on that file, which was to be your passport to glory and promotion."

I could tell Shaw was furious, inwardly boiling with anger. This was potentially disastrous for his career if Washington got to hear of it. He should have consulted his superiors, but was not sure of their refusal on political grounds, so he'd taken a chance. He must have thought me a clever bastard, getting him over this barrel... he has to get off somehow....

As calmly as he could manage, replied, "I knew they would turn it down, it was useless putting it to them."

"Maybe, but don't you see what a jam you're now in? Drury's dead *and* you don't have that precious file. Some will argue that you are responsible for Drury's death. Some may say by design."

"For Christ's sake, why would I want Drury dead?" cried Shaw in a cracked voice, a sign of one in fear.

"How would I know? I'm only painting the picture, not making historical and political judgement."

Shaw was visibly shaken. He asked in a whisper, "You really think it looks like that?"

I turned the ignition key and hit the starter with my boot. I pushed the lever into first and pulled away. Looking straight ahead into the night, I smiled a secret smile. Shaw was now malleable.

"You know bloody well it does," I asserted. "But don't worry. If you don't try your brand of deception on me, I won't let on...if you do, I'll kill you! Let's go, see what Club 46 has to offer."

7

BY THE THIRD day the mission was in full swing. Saigon's people reopened their shops and offices, spirits were lifted as business activity gained momentum. Some were actually sweeping the pavement in front of their shops and washing the windows, something they'd not done during the occupation.

Freedom's joy was seen in every face as work resumed. Something else was evident: pre-war relationships between the French and their colonial employees would never be the same. The French had been kicked out by the Japs and were thereby devalued as a great colonial power: they had lost face, dishonourable in Asian values.

Even more dishonourable was fraternising with the enemy. Those who had were marked for vengeance treatment and went in fear of those seeking retribution.

There could be no return to old colonial attitudes; the definitive hard line between master and servant was gone. A new spirit was abroad: nationalism was strong and the old name Annam was dropped in favour of Vietnam.

Nationalist groups formed on open spaces, defaming

French expatriates whom they claimed to be responsible for the war they believed must come.

The wise among expatriate French were well aware of this; alas, there were many blinkered by tradition and prejudice who would never see the obvious. Many, influenced by news that de Gaulle still dreamed of empire, blinded themselves to the misery that was inevitable.

The huge Chinese community controlling much of the country's commerce were apprehensive of this talk of nationalism. They knew it would spell their end if Ho Chi-minh got independence and practised his passion for ethnic purification.

Intelligence coming from Hunter and May told of communist activities during the occupation. Infiltration from Hanoi by Ho Chi-minh's experts in political persuasion had gone unchecked, despite Japanese counter-action. Ho himself had made many visits without detection, and established sleeper cells, now well organised and ready to create disruption when called upon.

Stafford May had irrefutable proof of a complete underground network of communist spies and agitators, silently awaiting call to action. As none of this was known to the civilian French, revelries went on pulsating to the joys of new-found freedom in blissful ignorance of the sinister dangers menacing their fragile security.

Miraculously, from secret hiding places never discovered by the Japanese, every kind of liquor and wine was now produced for the daily cocktail and dinner parties held in private homes and officers' messes, essential to post-occupation social recovery. British officers, regarded by the French as saviours of their land and way of life, became popular guests at all soirees. I found myself with more invitations than time would allow.

A healthy black market in short-supply goods, silk stockings and perfumes, thrived. Dr Eddie Blitz was reported active in most things, particularly brand-name spirits, Havana cigars and petrol. The enterprising Chinese, too, were into everything with startling results. Gordon's gin and Johnnie Walker whisky, along with numerous luxuries, unseen for years, became abundantly available as gifts for official favours. Most of these luxuries arrived by ships of all visiting navies. The Americans, through their PX Store, supplied more unusual items, such as the latest fashion in female underwear, and exotic perfumes.

Although French cocktail and dinner parties were scintillating moments of human intercourse, for sheer splendour the rich Chinese could outshine them, both in culinary art and the beauty of those tending at table— and to every desire a guest might afterwards have!

Days and nights of hectic happiness ensued as a hunger for pleasure gripped the people. Eager to savour every moment lest some new tragedy befall them, cavortings became one continuous pursuit of something more pleasurable than already experienced.

While all this went on, the famous French General Le Clere arrived with his staff, as agreed by the Allied Chiefs of Staff at Potsdam. This, according to the world's press, had to mean the French were indicating a preparedness to fight, if necessary. Le Clere became renowned as a fighting general—particularly with tanks—during the European war.

Officially it was a risky appointment because this general was much senior in rank to Major-General Gracey, under whom he would serve. Diplomatic concern had been voiced over this and, but for General Le Clere's magnanimity, a more junior general would have been appointed.

This gesture, played up by the press, enhanced his standing as soldier-statesman, earning him respect from military and civilians alike. However, it fuelled speculation that he was there for something more than diplomacy.

A complicated timetable had been prepared to enable progressive handover procedures from British to French authority but, due to squabbles between French senior civil servants, very little progress had been made. British authorities counted on Le Clere's prestige to change things, but jealousies abounded over appointments, as did resentment when it was discovered that certain officials had unsavoury political backgrounds.

The shadow of Vichy hung long and dark. Accusations of perfidy flew fiercely on airs of passion, from those patriots who loved la belle France. Some refused to serve with, or under, others deemed unworthy.

Le Clere's firmness was severely tested as courts of enquiry dealt with complaints, returning to France all whose wartime activities were suspect. Replacements of well screened officials arrived who, it was hoped, would quickly acclimatise, allowing a temporary transfer of administrative responsibility to be accelerated.

No sooner was this running smoothly than French press reports spoke of serious discord between British and French. Knowing this to be exaggerated, I set about tracing those responsible. I soon discovered that, among other purely imagined grievances, a small group maliciously made trouble over Le Clere's seniority to a British general who had command. Leaks of high-grade information from the Joint Committee also occurred. I had positive proof that unauthorised persons had news of secret discussions on possible partitioning for Vietnam, placing Emperor Bao-Dai on the throne in the south, and Ho Chi-minh in the north.

"A tricky situation," I said, reporting to Major-General Gracey, "British Intelligence checking out a French security problem would further impair relations between Britain and France."

"Very worrying," the general concurred. "Better get Bain in on this. He's very clever with delicate situations like this, calling for the diplomatic approach."

Peter Bain agreed that it was not an easy task for British investigators. "We must alert Le Clere and get his help," he said. "Imagine the resistance and hostility our people would meet. We'd get nowhere."

Major-General Gracey watched his political adviser, scratched his head, and decided to take his advice.

"OK," he accepted, "sounds right to me. You agree, Andrew?"

I nodded.

∝

British Signals Engineers finally established communications between Field Security HQ and my office, making life easier, with communications quicker and more secure. Most valuable adjunct was the intercom, enabling departments instant, safe contact with each other.

The corporal handed me the phone as I entered the outer office. "Captain Hunter for you, sir. Says there's a Professor Lien asking to see you."

"Tell him to hang on," I said, going into my own office, from which I re-emerged with a manila folder. The name on the cover was Professor Lien Cheong-leng, PhD.

I quickly refreshed my mind on the broad background of this brilliant, agile man. A socialist believing in equality of opportunity. In student days he had charm, balance, tolerance, and concern for the other fellow's point of view. At one time he expounded that to be an all-out communist was to enter the area of the "cloud cuckoo". It puzzled me how he finally became a communist. No doubt his meeting with Mao Tse-tung was responsible, made more so when he met and fell in love with Mao's beautiful and energetic disciple Soong Ping-min. There was an old photograph of Lien taken in 1939, but good enough, I decided.

Picking up the phone, I asked Hunter, "Does he want to see me there, or somewhere else?"

"He'll wait here for you. And come alone," Hunter stressed.

I hung up and pressed the intercom to tell the general, explaining the possible importance of talking with Professor Lien.

"Do you want Bain with you?" asked Gracey.

"Not this time, sir. He stipulates me alone."

Professor Lien, tall, slim and distinguished, fortyish, was alone in the room Hunter used as his office. Wearing black Chinese pyjamas and sandals, he sat dejectedly. He stood up as I entered, giving the traditional greeting. I asked for some identity, though I could see the likeness matched the photo. Lien produced a document bearing his photograph and signed by Lin Shao-chi, one of Mao's deputies.

"Who do you speak for?" I asked.

"Mao Tse-tung."

I took Hunter's chair at the desk while Lien resumed his seat.

"What can I do for you?" I asked, studying the visitor and trying to penetrate the mask so as to understand this man who might play an important role in the unfolding events of this troubled country

Speaking in flawless English, with only a slight problem with his Rs, Professor Lien began: "We understand that a decision has been taken to place Emperor Bao-Dai on the throne of Vietnam. We take this to mean a resumption of French colonial control. I am to say that this will lead to trouble for two reasons: Ho Chi-minh will not accept it; nor will China."

"What has all this to do with Mao Tse-tung?"

"Civil war will be disastrous for Chinese nationals throughout Indo-China. And should Russian influence be established, our nationals will be purged."

"What are you asking?" I demanded.

"That the Allied governments realise the folly of this, and make an arrangement with Ho Chi-minh and Chiang Kai-shek for joint control of Indo-China. There is no other way of preventing war. Ho-Chi-minh would agree to this in exchange for certain economic and political guarantees."

"How can we make sure Ho will agree, and General Chiang Kai-shek?"

"Under proper safeguards a meeting could be arranged with Ho Chi-minh, and General Chiang's approval can be established to your satisfaction."

I was curious on one apparent, irreconcilable point: "I find it strange that you, a communist, should plead for Chiang Kai-shek, your ideological enemy!"

Allowing a thin smile a moment's life, Lien reminded me that Chiang was as much an ally as Russia, whereas Mao Tse-tung had no standing yet. "And," he went on, "Chiang is a reformer too, we have much in common. Besides, Chiang's reign will end in a few years, then we will be in power. It is imperative to keep Russia out of Indo-China. You will know, major, there's a price to pay for everything. We do not want Russia on our southern flank, and we are sure Britain will oppose it having regard to her Malayan interests."

Already alarmed that information about French intentions to restore Bao-Dai to the throne was being leaked from the Joint Council, here was additional evidence. Either someone high up has spoken out of turn, or perfidiously. Security certainly needed review: this was a French responsibility, procedural difficulties would make it impossible for me to plug the hole.

The professor's proposal was, of course, a good one, but neither the French nor the Russians would agree. He was right about British Malayan interests—a strong point. Lien had not mentioned the Americans, probably because he knew they would only agree to France holding sway in Indo-China.

"Let's waste no time, professor. Bring us confirmation that Ho Chi-minh will agree to a meeting—at what level, the terms, and where to hold it. We'll need proof that

General Chiang Kai-shek will work with Ho Chi-minh. You will see that these matters are vital if agreement to the meeting is to be possible. Chiang and Ho have not always been friends."

Lien agreed and we said goodbye, the professor promising to act quickly.

❧

To Hunter, who appeared as our visitor was let out, I gave the task of checking on the leak of information from the Joint Council, having decided that the gravity of the situation warranted risking offending the French.

"Go very carefully on this," I warned, "it's a French matter really, we mustn't be too obvious. I know this won't be easy and we may have to use Gracey's name if questions are asked. I'll speak to him and maybe we can get Le Clere's blessing."

❧

Professor Lien's startlingly dramatic proposal sets my mental and emotional mechanisms racing. I want to get into the rhythm of preparatory planning, sounding out those who matter, who must be informed and so on. But I can't tell the general, Gracey would kill the thing then and there.

First, I must consult Peter Bain. The word "deception" forms firmly in my mind. I'm thinking ahead with boldness and audacity – I'll deceive the general rather than let this golden opportunity wither.

Too many questions and thoughts tend to cloud the issue. I look for Peter Bain, first trying the obvious – his office.

"Not sure where he's gone," said the clerk. "I think he'll be back soon."

No sooner was I back in my own office than the phone rang with Peter Bain saying: "You want me, Andrew?"

"Yes, can you come to me?" I had to have privacy.

I explained it all very carefully, leaving nothing out; but was guarded over the emotional emphasis so as not to influence Peter Bain's judgement.

Bain's face registered a mixture of messages; clearly he was thrilled, as was I. But facial expression became glum at the suggestion of deception and he burst out, "No! Forget it, Andrew. I know how opposed you are to French restoration to government. I feel the same, now. The best thing is to wait and see how things turn out. I'm sure these poor sods are in for a rough time. War *will* come and you were right when you earlier predicted the outcome. Ho *will* win with the aid of China and Russia supplying weapons and economic aid; remember… you said it was a Sino-Russian problem?

"I recall a Chinese saying that fits this situation beautifully. 'You can't fart against thunder.' There's no way of altering the course of history… there's going to be bloody civil war for certain. It doesn't matter if you tell the general; the part he plays will be his undoing. As you say, Andrew, the remarkable thing is the communist request for the nationalists' benefit."

"It's either a giant public-relations ploy or genuine concern for the Chinese in Cholon, Cambodia and Laos," I observed, remembering my conversation with Eddie Blitz. "Of course the strategic consideration is powerful. No one wants Russia calling the tune in Indo-China, threatening Siam, Malaya, Singapore locally—even Australia and New Zealand, long term."

8

COMMISSION HQ BECAME the political and social sieve, through which both major and minor problems were processed. Peter Bain's skills were usually capable of diplomatic treatment with a high degree of success. It was normal for matters affecting the civil population to be referred to the French as and when they were set up to cope; liaison was gradually developing, leaving areas of administrative difficulty that no one was aptly qualified to act on. In such cases the commission did its best to find acceptable, though by no means total, solutions.

One such problem concerned General Lu-han, the nationalist Chinese general appointed by the Allied Chiefs of Staff to disarm Japanese troops in Indo-China, north of sixteen-degree parallel. Admiral Mountbatten, affectionately known as SAC, is anxious to have the warlord general, Lu-han, remove himself and his army from Indo-China in compliance with an order issued by the Potsdam Conference.

Warlords historically are a law unto themselves; they resent being told what to do; it is not in their nature, for one thing, but is particularly objectionable since warlords *give orders* and lesser mortals *obey*. To do otherwise would result in loss of face and automatic loss of authority: warlords then become ordinary beings, a status none will accept. The correct approach to a warlord is by request, sweetened with generous flattery and incentives.

Mountbatten, therefore, asked Gracey to use Major Grant to find out why Lu-han had not complied with a diplomatic request made earlier. It is vitally important that General Lu-han, with his entire army, should leave the territory. Every effort must be made to get him to go.

Gracey explained the problem to me, indicating the line Lord Louis suggested. "I don't want to send you, Andrew, for obvious reasons, with all you have on your plate, but there's no one else. You're the only one who speaks his language, I believe. They tell me he only uses Mandarin. Can you spare a couple of days?"

I chuckled at this and the general raised his eyebrows questioningly.

"What's so funny?"

"This can't be done in a couple of days, sir. Lu-han won't even *see* me for forty-eight hours, then he'll deliberately let me cool my heels for another day. After that the preliminaries begin; these could take another day, at least. He'll be in no hurry. I suspect he's there with Ho Chi-minh's blessing."

"Bloody hell! But it has to be done, we must find out what's bugging him. I'll send him a signal now requesting the visit and see what he replies. And by the way, he won't talk to anyone under the rank of general, so you will become a brigadier for the purpose and I want you to take Captain Winton, RN, with you, as a mission. He'll be dressed as a commodore, I think he speaks Cantonese."

A neat piece of diplomatic deception, permissible in these circumstances.

☙

Winton and I were received in style at Hanoi Airport. A military band played the British and Chinese national anthems and another piece taken to be that of Vietnam. Senior officers of General Lu-han's army made welcoming speeches, inviting their guests to inspect the guard of honour. After formal ceremonies were diplomatically concluded, a splendid limousine resembling the kind used by senior French colonial governors, and driven by a Chinese soldier, carried us to a palatial mansion on the outskirts of Hanoi City.

In the spacious grounds were many buildings well away from the august mansion used as Lu-han's military headquarters; a vast complex providing officers' messes and accommodation for troops permanently guarding the general.

We are welcomed by a resplendently attired Chinese, the equivalent of a Spanish major-domo, the chief official of the general's household. Charm and courtesy are dispensed as we are shown to our rooms. Here we find two personal servants, one of each sex, both young and very attractive.

Their responsibilities, it is explained, are to serve and please. "They will bath and dress you, bring refreshments or anything else. You only have to ask."

Alone, at last, admiring the splendour of our bedrooms, we found difficulty taking it all in. Never had either of us before experienced such lavish extravagance of generosity. It was overwhelming.

Although we thoroughly enjoyed the luxury, we realised the purpose was to flatter and disarm. There could be but one simple meaning: Lu-han had no intention of leaving. Our job, therefore, was plain: to find out why he wouldn't—or couldn't—withdraw.

A reassessment of our position, skills and assets, reveals that Winton speaks only enough Cantonese and Hockien to understand roughly what is being said. I'll have to prompt him in coded English as necessary and hopefully he will be able to make an intelligent contribution if we are drawn into conversation.

✩

We experience a remarkable four days.

Entertainment lavishly provided by this wily old warrior is to be savoured before formally presenting Admiral Mountbatten's request for Lu-han to withdraw.

A sequence of polite social intercourse is necessary before any business discussions can commence. Such was the custom, an aide explained. A ritual or rite, as prelude to formalities.

The general played the perfect host. Female companions surpassed anything ever before imagined. Guests would find it difficult to deny themselves the sensual pleasures filling the hours of waiting for Lu-han's readiness to parley. We were no exception—it would have been unmanly to refuse.

Our attendants were as slaves to their temporary masters, themselves leading the way to pleasures not experienced before with such artistry and satisfaction.

On the third day, there is a change from the exotic festivities—the general decided to be classical. It was time to display his wonderful collection of works of art.

This proved the reputation of Lu-han as a "collector". He had filled three huge rooms with every conceivable art form—of astonishing beauty: not only Chinese and Japanese but of Western culture—all dubiously acquired!

Throughout this exceptionally beautiful display of art, in many forms, the general was remarkably erudite concerning his treasures. I think he'd mugged up on them so as to impress.

Winton and I were attracted to a group of unbelievably beautiful, life-size marble statues of nude young men and women. The work was described by a Chinese woman, who claimed to be expert in marble carving, as of Italian creation about 200 years old.

We stood admiring the piece, believing the work to be authentic, when, at the snap of the woman's fingers the figures came alive in poetic movement and dance.

It was the prelude to erotic lovemaking. Though shocked and surprised, we both had to admit this, too, was art of the highest calibre on two counts: firstly, of astonishment—as that which appeared inanimate suddenly became vitally alive; secondly, the erotic display was of classical art to the extent that we became spectators, not voyeurs.

Of course, to the general and other Chinese who had seen it before there was humour for those of broader mind. We had to admit to finding it amusing, too.

Lu-han was attentive to detail, ensuring that our glasses were topped up while pretty young Chinese girls, in colourful cheongsams, served canapés.

Eventually I signalled to Winton, pointing to my watch. We both thanked the general and left to freshen up for lunch in an hour's time.

"I guess we'll have to be leaving in the morning," was

my gloomy forecast to Winton. "I can find no reason to prolong our visit; nothing we can say will persuade Lu-han to leave. I think he's done a deal with Ho Chi-minh."

We assembled in a small lounge beside the dining room for pre-lunch appetisers served by the same lovelies as at the art show.

General Lu-han arrived with three men, one in uniform, and immediately latched on to me as being the man to get to know better.

He was in good spirits, chuckling or loudly laughing at his own jocular remarks. "Lunch is a time for eating and talking business, is it not, brigadier?"

"Sure," I agreed, "that's why we're here. I'm looking forward to our discussions, as I'm certain my friend the commodore is."

Lu-han used this moment to introduce his other guests. These proved to be a lawyer, a politician and a soldier. "My advisers," he explained. "They will answer technical questions and help me on points of law."

The dining room is of startling beauty, its walls hung with silk, hand-woven tapestries depicting Chinese hunting scenes. Furniture in the classical style of exquisitely carved dragons, the rich wood gleaming.

"Made of rosewood," Lu-han explained. "It's much lighter than the hard woods."

Lovely silk rugs were scattered over ochre-coloured wood flooring, giving to the room richness and beauty.

Lu-han opened the formal discussions after the second

course of swallow's nest with special soup; the first course being the most favourite starter, shark's fin soup.

Food was served by our personal servants who, after placing a meal on the table in front of us, stood behind our chairs while we ate, ready to provide condiments or anything else we might desire: sheer luxury. Our two servants worked in relays, waiting on us exclusively.

Lu-han thanked us for coming with Lord Louis's request. No fool, this warlord general: he is aware of the diplomatic subtleties. He is jovial, his beaming smile becomes a musical laugh as he continues to speak. "If only you knew how difficult this is, I'm sure Lord Louis would understand."

This was an opening gambit, I thought, to what sounded like a conditioner for the nasty bit to follow.

I took this early opportunity to remind Lu-han that we were conveying a request from the joint Chiefs of Staff. "Lord Louis is merely passing the order on to Your Excellency," I said, hoping this elevated title might help diplomatically. "I'm sure Lord Louis would like to know of your problems. He naturally thinks your responsibilities ceased after disarming the Japanese," I ventured.

To my surprise, the general opened up with, "Good, that's what I hoped you'd say. Now let me explain. I have entered into many business deals that compel me to remain here to honour my obligations.

"There are intricate political problems, too, regarding Ho Chi-minh and myself. I have agreed to assist His Excellency in his plans to prevent the French taking control in the north of the country. Ho Chi-minh has agreed to include some Chinese in the administration of North Vietnam. And, finally, he has asked my help in collecting a great deal of gold hidden by the people of Hanoi. Ho Chi-minh has persuaded the Hanoi population to donate this gold to his depleted treasury. Based on my understanding of Lord Louis I'm sure he will be sympathetic to my request for a stay of departure."

He paused, realised food was not being served and ordered it to be resumed. Asparagus and mushrooms with fried chicken in the Peking style followed, to everybody's delight. Then sea fish and fried rice of Yangchow City, coffee and brandy: a sumptuous meal.

"What do you think, brigadier?" asked Lu-han, as if pleading, which is unusual in a warlord. "Will that impress Lord Louis?"

I was inwardly laughing for I knew it would definitely impress everybody who came to hear of it. It was a *fait accompli*—nothing more to say.

"Yes, general, he certainly will be impressed!"

At this point, Lu-han, speaking in a dialect unknown to me, addressed his legal guest in quiet conversation. Returning to Mandarin he apologised for using a dialect and explained, "I asked my friend a legal question not so easily expressed in Mandarin. I asked him if there was a legal reason in international law why I may not remain here longer to assist Ho Chi-minh. He thinks not, since I am staying on at His Excellency's request."

I thanked him for this explanation. As I thought, Lu-han had done a deal with Ho Chi-minh and there was nothing could be done about it.

Conversation sparkled as Lu-han expanded, telling of his long march from China with over 200,000 troops and 6,000 dependants—mostly concubines.

"You call them 'comfort girls', I believe?"

Neither I nor Winton made any comment. No purpose would be served. We both smiled our understanding.

Our host was particularly anxious to explain why he occupied a mansion. "It demonstrates my popularity with all types of people here. This splendid palace," as he described it, "has been made available to me by a Mandarin."

As an afterthought he explained another reason for not leaving the territory. Ho Chi-minh had asked his help in harvesting the opium crop in Laos. "As this will not be ready to harvest for nearly one year I feel obliged to remain to assist His Excellency."

Something about the way he told the story sounded phoney. He'd put up a splendid show, presenting an image of total honesty. He obviously thought his British guests greenhorns who knew nothing of the ways of the warlord class.

Apart from that learnt through history lessons, when warlords are grandiose warriors, brutal but brave—even heroic—more intense reading reveals them as land pirates, murderers, cut-throats, marauding pillagers.

General Lu-han had this reputation. Above all else he would not want popularity from local people; rather, he would create fear, by which he could take whatever he wanted. The last thing he'd take would be charity.

A mixed result to our visit but at least we now knew of the reasons for Lu-han refusing to leave.

"Not good news for Mountbatten," I said to Winton. "If the French come to hear of it they'll be worried, to learn of Lu-han's military support of Ho Chi-minh."

With all the usual courtesies we took our leave the next day. We knew that to parley further would serve no good purpose.

While we were away, Professor Lien had delivered the message to Hunter, who gave it to me on my return.

Major-General Gracey was amused to learn that Lu-han would not withdraw his forces until he had transported fifty tons of gold from the territory, together with the opium crop from Laos.

"We'd never get away with that, would we?" he chuckled. "It's old-time stuff, spoils to the victor. How long does he need for all this looting?"

"No way of knowing, sir," I replied. "As I measure it, the opium will be the factor. Gold doesn't have to ripen! The best estimate is between one and two years—even longer. As I see it, Ho Chi-minh has use of Lu-han's army, to fight such battles as may be instigated by the French. I'm of the opinion Lu-han will become part of Ho Chi-minh's military answer to the French. In which case he'll be there for many years."

The general watched as I opened a folded paper. "What's that?" he asked.

"Professor Lien's message saying he will call at Hunter's place tonight at 2200 hours, with confirmation of willing participation by Mao Tse-tung and Chiang Kai-shek in our plan for some form of independence for Ho Chi-minh."

"OK, Andrew. Something's happening right. You'll let me know the outcome as a matter of urgency? And by the way, my recommendation for your promotion has been approved by Admiral Mountbatten. So, when you're taking pips from your shoulder straps, leave one with the crown, lieutenant-colonel."

I smiled my thanks, inwardly elated. I saluted and left the room.

9

WHEN I REACHED my office, Chief Superintendent Deshampneuf was waiting in the outer room. He had just arrived from France to replace Aubaire, he explained. His English was halting and not fluent enough for easy conversation.

I replied in impeccable Parisian French, to the relief and surprise of the superintendent.

"Oh, my!" Deshampneuf said, unbelieving. "You speak like a Frenchman!"

"Nice of you to call," I said. "Anything special to discuss?"

"No, colonel. I just want to say hello and offer co-operation in any way."

I thanked him and, to show willing, said, "Please call me at any time. I'll contact you at Sureté when necessary. By the way, were you here pre-war?"

"Yes, I was here for four years, and went on leave just before the Japs invaded."

"So you knew Aubaire?"

"I was his junior."

"Sad," I commiserated, "being killed by a snake."

"I expect he was drunk, as usual, so he wouldn't have felt it. I don't want to sound disrespectful or callous towards the dead, colonel, but he was very much under suspicion of communist activity before the war, and would have been arrested and sent home if Special Branch had completed their investigation in time."

"Very interesting," I remarked, knowing that others knew all about Aubaire's activities.

"We thought you'd like to know this, colonel. As a matter of fact, his death has saved us much embarrassment and expense."

I smiled as I closed the door on the chief superintendent, thinking it was nice of him to come and say thank you for disposing of a problem for them.

Still speculating on this encounter, I swung my jeep out through the officers' mess gateway and along the back streets, dark and almost deserted, and turned left for Hunter's place, on the western side of the cathedral.

Professor Lien was in the office as before, but in brighter mood. I read the message signed by Ho Chi-minh, as President of the Republic of Vietnam, and General Chiang Kai-shek. It contained four points:

1 We agree to meet with Admiral Mountbatten
   to explore the possibility of making an
   arrangement for setting up a Sino-Vietnamese
   administration in Vietnam with supervision
   by Britain and another friendly power, other
   than Russia.

2 Meeting to take place at a convenient venue with airstrip and suitably secure building nearby.

3 Not more than one aide to a side.

4 This note must be destroyed by burning in front of Professor Lien.

I memorised the contents and burnt the paper, dropping the flaming remnant into a tin ashtray.

"You realise," I started to explain, "that several days will be required before an answer can be given? Comprehensive discussion must be conducted with Admiral Mountbatten in Singapore; this means personal contact by me, which will require at least seven days."

Lien was not surprised and nodded his approval, adding, "But please make it as few days as possible, colonel."

I promised to do what I could, and the professor slipped away into the dark and humid night.

I dialled the general's number, hoping to catch him in.

"No," said Sergeant Fagge, "he's at the Le Cleres' for dinner, said he would be late."

"What... again!?" I exclaimed. "He's getting very pally with Le Clere. This must be the fourth time this month."

I decided that the morning would do, and hung up. I wanted a woman. I wanted Maryse.

I poured a large scotch into an ice-cold glass, allowed a bare five seconds for it to chill slightly, then threw it back. My thoughts switched to work. Grading the Japanese was going well but I was sure many in the "black" category would cheat us through lack of evidence and witnesses. Freddie Coombes, in charge of Engineers, should have reported progress on the erection of the stand for the Japanese surrender parade. I made a note to call him. I wondered how Hunter was making out with the security check, and what Stafford May had achieved with the communist spy network.

Thinking again about Lu-han, his fifty tons of gold and the opium crop, I grinned. Only a warlord could get away with something like this. How long, I wondered, would the Chinese warlord class survive? Judging by Professor Lien's remark, only a few more years. How would Lord Louis react to Ho's proposal? I wondered, too, about Lu-han's subtle aside when we were alone together; the words seemed to connect with Lien's remark. Lu-han had said that where he was soon to go much money would be required for one of his rank!

At 1100 hours I left the apartment for the Rue Colombier. "Who knows?" I thought, forcing the jeep to produce unaccustomed speed for so short a journey, "I might take that pipe of opium tonight."

10

RESPONDING TO A request for urgent consultation, I went to the general's office where the genial Sergeant Fagge, clutching a bundle of files, stood wearing an odd expression on his normally lively, smiling face. There was something whimsical about it, even a little naughty.

As I regarded this visit a routine affair, I found this picture of Fagge, the general's confidential and unflappable clerk, somewhat mystifying. Suddenly a capricious smile consumed the cloudy countenance and at once a new puzzle developed from Fagge's whispered "Good luck, sir" as he opened the communicating door to the inner office; a wink further deepened the mystery.

"Ah," said Gracey, "there you are, Andrew. Come and meet Captain Barbancourt."

A smart and strikingly handsome young woman stood up, saluted and offered her hand, which I took in the French fashion. She registered surprise that an Englishman would show such courteous use of French custom.

I noted the uniform did nothing to conceal her shapeliness; on the contrary, against all that was normal, it actually revealed curves that demanded appreciation.

"Sit down and relax," added the general, noting my obvious approval of the visitor. "Captain Barbancourt is here to help you with the business of the leak at the Joint Council. General Le Clere arranged this as they have no qualified personnel available locally. She has come direct from Paris."

I was speculating about Suzie Barbancourt; mainly about her origins, for clearly she was not pure anything. The colour of the skin was neither white nor brown. The eyes were startlingly dark and misty, like black pearls; while the hair, mostly hidden under a forage cap and shining like black satin, was dressed in a knot resting on the nape of a graceful neck. The features were Caucasian and perfect in the classical sense, yet there was a duskiness of complexion that argued against this.

The general broke my reverie with, "Now, Andrew, stop your speculating."

I smiled, as if being caught out and mildly scolded. "You know me too well, sir."

"Now, to put you in the picture. Suzie comes from Haiti where the family have lived since 1765. She's lived in France from her early school days and, after university, joined the French Corps Diplomatique. It's all in this file Suzie brought with her. You can have it after I've told you how clever she is." The general enjoyed saying this. "To complement her many accomplishments in languages, she has a perfect photo-memory *and* she's expert at disguise."

"Sounds too good to be true," I said, returning the smile, "but since you say so, I believe."

Suzie watched this by-play and no doubt decided that a few chosen words for this cocky colonel, of whom she'd been fully clued in, might be appropriate.

A rich, full musical voice, always a delight to the ear, more particularly from one so intriguing as Suzie Barbancourt. Several tones lower than the normal female voice and a shade husky, it charmed her listeners, as she explained.

"My screening started in London and continued at Singapore, ending here in General Le Clere's office. My briefing originated in Paris, to be continued here by General Le Clere, and, as I understand it, you, colonel, will complete the picture for me."

"Bon. I'll not only do that, but I'll complete your screening as well."

Suzie smiled and I wondered about her in more ways than one; while the general, speculating about the future of these two attractive and highly efficient young people, made a small and silent bet with himself (as he confided in me at a later date) that I had met my match in Suzie Barbancourt. Even so, he felt sure that I would ultimately win.

"You see, Andrew!" he said with emphasis. "Good, isn't she?"

"Almost too good to be true," I countered with my usual banter and ostensible fun. "Who knows she's here other than General Le Clere, Fagge and us?"

"No one," Suzie intruded, "and not even General Le Clere would recognise me as I am now. I was a reporter in civilian clothes with a different hairstyle when I delivered a letter of introduction from Admiral d'Argenlieu, which was good enough for General Le Clere."

"Splendid." I pretended to be impressed. "When did you arrive?"

"By military plane yesterday afternoon, along with a couple of journalists."

"Where did you stay last night?"

"In the Press Hostel."

"How did you manage to change into uniform without being seen by the journalists?"

Gracey studied this exchange, enjoying every thrust and parry. At this point his eyebrows rose apprehensively. He looked at her awaiting a reply. She paused, and for a moment he thought she was stumped. So did I, beginning to have doubts as to her real purpose in Saigon. The general shifted in his chair, turning more to face her as if willing her to answer satisfactorily, and trying to hide the disappointment beginning to cloud his rugged face.

"This was a bit tricky," she began, sensing that both of us had begun wondering about her. "I only changed into uniform because my instructions told me to when presenting myself to Major-General Gracey. But for this I would still be a reporter. As you know, the press can go anywhere without attracting too much attention. I made the change in the public toilets in the theatre." She pointed to a holdall by her chair. "My civilian clothes are in there."

I was still puzzled that she had to report to the general personally. In the British army a mere captain would report to me, but I had to admit this was a different setting.

Clearly relieved, the general hastened to introduce normality. "How about a drink, and after lunch you two can continue your business."

98

During the meal I decided how we could work together. I thought it best to let her loose, to come up with whatever she could find.

This suited her. "I work best that way. All we need is an arrangement for me to report safely. We must have a coding for messages and identities. I never refer to places, subjects or individuals by name."

"That's fine, but what about accommodation?"

"I'll fend for myself. In this way I fade into the landscape better in whatever role I choose to play. I need nothing beyond reporting facilities, contact arrangements like phone numbers, dropping-off points and so on. Of course, codes—I'll need these. Beyond this, there's your final briefing and I'm ready to go."

I could almost have been listening to an English girl, just a trace of accent was discernible to my sensitive ear, it was the subtlest lilt of the Caribbean.

I suggested we run through my file on the case that evening. "I have appointments until 1630 hours. We'll set up the system and have a dummy run on each phase. Coding will be the kind we can memorise—OK?"

"The simpler the better, as long as it has a daily variable," she agreed. "The first thing is to get out of this uniform."

"You can do that in my office," I said with a smile.

Suzie smiled back and the general raised his eyebrows but said nothing.

I handed Gracey my report on Lien's proposal as Suzie and I left together.

I learnt something of Haitian passion that night. I learnt much, too, about Suzie. Here was something special.

We made love in French, garnished here and there with delicious intimacies in Creole, which Suzie naughtily explained. She knew the art of suspense and played her lovemaking as I did stud poker: under tension, delaying the moments of surrender and victory.

As we lay recovering, we smoked, relaxing from our exertions. It was almost unbearably humid, and a bead of sweat wriggled down my nose, falling onto the cigarette with a fizzing sound, and disappearing in a tiny puff of steam.

Suzie looked at me and drew her hand from my thigh as she turned, resting on one elbow.

Taking the cigarette from lips still swollen from passionate kisses, she said softly and slowly, "Andrew, mon chéri," in a voice stumbling here and there, out of step with her thoughts.

I looked at her thinking that her speech was strange, and wondering if she was all right.

"What is it, honey?" I used an Americanism I thought apt in this odd situation.

She pulled long on her cigarette, inhaled deeply and blew the smoke from lips forming a small opening, making rings. She stubbed out the butt thinking how to say, "I haven't come clean with you," she began.

"Over what?"

"Well... I have another assignment apart from identifying the leak of information. It's nothing to do with you really, but after tonight, I think it's best to tell you about it."

"So," I invited flippantly, "what can it be—other than to keep me company in bed?"

"That's a bonus," she said, kissing my mouth, "and it's part of the deal. But, seriously, mon chéri, my main task is finding out why Ho Chi-minh has stopped talking to us. Investigating the leak is only my cover."

This triggered my alert mechanism and thoughts tumbled around as I pondered this revelation. Did she know something or, maybe, simply suspect? Care was needed. Funny how, at the general's office, I had thought her unusually well qualified for a routine job of tracing a leak. I decided to attack.

"How do you mean, Ho has stopped talking to you? I didn't know you people had something going with Ho. You doing some kind of a deal behind our back?"

"Naturally we are. There's no way we can just carry on as if nothing has happened," she said with force. "Ho has to be reckoned with. We're not going behind your back. It's *our* affair."

"OK," I said, to calm things. "I see that. But would it not be wise to tell us what's going on? We might, through ignorance of your plans, unwittingly spoil things for you."

"I see that, but that's up to Admiral d'Argenlieu, who arrives tomorrow. I'll mention it to General Le Clere and he can decide."

"Have you no clue as to why Ho stopped talking?"

"None. He just broke off by not appearing at an arranged meeting, and all attempts to contact him have failed."

"If you want some help, just say so," I offered, content that I now knew the score. I decided to make further enquiries about this fascinating female who, by this admission, had more to her than was officially announced.

Suzie slipped away in the early morning, a tatty-looking thing bearing no resemblance to the sex kitten I had devoured for most of the night. Her mixed blood was an asset, but her skills with wigs and makeup were masterly.

I made coffee while grabbing a handful of biscuits. A shave and shower and I was ready for the day. My watch said 0910 hours as I entered my office through the private door. Time to write up my notes for the ten o'clock meeting. Time, too, to recap the general situation.

I was interrupted by Eddie Blitz knocking and poking his cream-coloured face round the door. Blitz attempted a smile and apologised for disturbing, his pale falsetto voice rising even higher than usual. He gave me a list of names with explanatory notes.

"I won't keep you now, Andrew. And, congratulations, *colonel*! Send me word when you've checked out this information. Have to dash."

As he left, May and Hunter appeared for routine reports and updating. Hunter, as always, painted the picture in clear and obvious style so the facts were exposed; his assessment of them left no one in doubt of the value to be given to each circumstance.

He had no doubt the French would have great difficulty restoring colonial systems to Indo-China. Information reaching his HQ through informants confirmed that the native population, other than the Chinese, wanted independence under Ho Chi-minh, their national hero.

"As for other things," he said, reflecting amazement in his voice, "I tell you, Andrew, the place is alive with intrigue. None of the normal rules apply—it's everyone for themselves! The French want this, the Annamites and the Chinese something else, and I'm certain there's no solution to this problem."

Stafford May was clearly at peace with life. He was doing

what he liked best: the chase, the thrill, even the risks were a tonic. In no time his unit had become fully operational. He had a smooth-running machine producing results. For his personal comfort a pretty young Annamite, full bosomed and warm hearted, had become his servant and pleasure.

His report, as always, was lucid and informative. He knew all about Dockland and of a meeting between four men—three Annamites and one Russian.

"I picked up the accent straightaway, though he spoke in Annamese," he said, as if to confirm my unspoken question. "I've got this one taped completely. I have him watched all the time. His three contacts, too. They called the Russian Boris. Must be the Ulowski Maryse told you about."

"Boris can't be up to any good, Stafford. Perhaps we should just take him out... before he gets too organised and spoils our plans!"

"Plenty of time for that," May replied, eager to use the man to his advantage. "He may produce something of value to us."

"Well, don't let him get too nosy. Once you've identified his cell members and made a pattern of their activities, he's to be quietly expended."

"OK, Andrew."

"I'll need Benoit in a day or two to assist Paul with the leak of information at the Joint Council. As soon as you can spare him, send him to me. He'll like this one. He's going to tail a lovely bird from his part of the world."

11

DEEP IN THE satellite town of Cholon a powerful group had gathered in a private room on the top floor of the Sun Wah Restaurant. They had come stealthily by secret routes from Hanoi in the north, heavily disguised and taking many a long detour so as to avoid being recognised.

Their purpose was to receive Professor Lien's report as part of the eventual takeover of Saigon City and the independence of Vietnam. While attaching much importance to the proposed meeting with Mountbatten, they were fully prepared with an alternative strategy, should nothing come of it.

The meeting was controlled by Ho Chi-minh, a slight man whose sharp aquiline features were softened by a wispy beard and long flowing moustache. Though aging, he was still the dynamic revolutionary, the old charisma unfaded. In student days he was a rebel determined to change things in his homeland. His studies took him abroad to many lands where he grew in stature, receiving recognition from leaders of socialist persuasion, and respect from others.

In England it was normal to find him washing dishes to supplement a meagre income from his many sympathisers. In France he enjoyed a scholarship with a small grant made possible by those who hoped to win him to another point of view. It was in Russia, however, that he found most assistance and political succour.

Always intensely republican, opposed to colonialism, and fiercely nationalistic, he had clashed with the French authorities before the war, and, like most of his breed, was no stranger to exile.

Now, as the revered leader of the Popular Front, he controlled a formidable army in camps spread about the country. He worked ceaselessly for the day when he would be installed as president of the independent state of Vietnam.

Attending the meeting were guerrilla communists: Chinese and Vietnamese; Marxists and Maoists. A mixed bag of rebels insinuating their style of revolution into their respective countries, China and Vietnam, with ambitions of extending their ideological influence to Cambodia and Laos. And, of course, ultimately to Siam, Malaya and Burma.

Vietnamese Chairman Ho Chi-minh, though sympathetic to the aims and aspirations of communism, was first and foremost a nationalist. His view was that colonialism was fundamentally wrong in concept and against all natural justice. He argued that nations should not be subservient to one another; that his people, so long dominated and exploited by the French, must be freed by any means— even bloody war.

So much was hanging on the success of this meeting, I arranged with Professor Lien Cheong-Leng to bring news of the outcome as soon afterwards as he could.

By arrangement I went to my flat on Rue Catinat to receive Professor Lien Cheong-Leng, whose report on the Sun Wah Restaurant meeting I awaited with some impatience.

I had Cheong Sie-Ling with me to help with drinks, his speciality; but more for atmosphere.

A coded tap on the door announced the arrival of the professor, who to my surprise wore Western clothes. He was smiling; mostly, I thought, at my own facial expression.

"You are surprised, colonel, as I hoped you would be... and pleasantly, I hope. This is, after all, the garb I adopted throughout my student days in Europe and the States: I feel more relaxed wearing it now, so as to remove barriers. We are friends embarked on a wonderful escapade of drama and hope!"

We shook hands warmly and I introduced Sie-Ling, as one of my team who would be very active in our plans.

"So, what did you drink in student days?" I asked.

"Many different kinds, but my favourite is scotch and ginger ale."

Sie-Ling did the honours and we sat ourselves down at a glass-topped table where lay snacks, made by Sie-Ling, who was a dab hand at social niceties.

"As you will know," I ventured, "your news of the meeting is awaited with bated breath. Did something good come out of it?"

A smile gradually broadened on Lien's handsome face, accompanied by an excited "Yes, it really did!" Then he paused. "I won't bore you with the preliminaries... the most important is a proposal that the rendezvous should be in the Grand Hotel at Siem Riap."

"Why there?" I asked. "Is it safe, would you say?"

"Is any place safe, colonel? All the delegates finally

agreed that because of its famous ruins at Angkor Wat it's a natural place for Lord Mountbatten to spend two or three days resting from his arduous duties in Singapore. It's as safe as any other place and can be made more safe by you and your Gurkha soldiers. Do you not agree?"

"It is a well known tourist attraction," Sie Ling offered. "The important factor is the degree of secrecy we employ to the plan and its implementation."

"Sounds fine," I added.

"We have a way of surreptitiously 'conditioning' the area," Lien Cheong-Leng elucidated, "that arouses no untoward excitement when news breaks that a famous person will be visiting."

"That settles it," was my final remark.

"Good. We'll be meeting many more times, so for now, goodbye, colonel." And Professor Lien Cheong-Leng arose, shook hands, and left.

The proposal for the meeting was, I thought, bold. I liked it. I poured scotch onto ice cubes and mulled over the possibilities of error and areas where, at this particular time, plans could not be finalised.

Well satisfied that the picture was clear, I left to join Major-General Gracey and Peter Bain as previously arranged.

"What a strange set-up," was the general's comment. "I agree, it's bold and good. But, even if Mountbatten agrees, will London?"

"Good question," Peter Bain replied. "If Lord Louis likes it we're halfway there. He's very persuasive, and has influence."

"What's London got to lose?" I asked. "If Mountbatten is willing and secrecy is maintained, they've all to gain."

Gracey was deep in thought, his eyes moving from one to the other. "That's it!" he said. "Secrecy! Andrew, you drop everything for twenty-four hours and put this proposition to the admiral personally. First make sure that SAC is in Singapore."

This left me further disturbed as to Gracey's true intentions. A strange uncomfortable relationship was developing between us. Obviously we were on diametrically different courses of action, the general to support a French takeover of the country as a colony; and me to thwart this by arranging a meeting between Mountbatten and Ho Chi-minh to discuss a form of independence for his country. There was a possibility that Gracey had heard of American support for the French. He sounded like a man with a secret! At the same time I got the impression that the general wanted a foot in both camps, in case one went wrong.

We are both aware of this cat-and-mouse game we are playing and naturally we are each convinced of success. In fact we've enjoyed the game of deception. We could not do otherwise.

I briefed myself thoroughly on the senior British officers I'd be likely to meet, knowing that the Mountbattens belonged in what was fashionably called the "progressive camp" and found that, in general terms, some were what I would regard as being of similar persuasion.

Lord Louis's father, Prince Louis of Battenburg, as First Sea Lord, had introduced into the Royal Navy unheard-of opportunities for the lower decks to attain officer status, and Lady Louis was the author of several left-wing articles, thus creating an influence politically to the left of centre, within the family.

I had no doubt that the Supreme Allied Commander would agree to the meeting, if only on grounds that he might be helping the underdog; certainly the possibility of civil war would influence his decision on humanitarian grounds. The question was: would the Prime Minister be prepared to take the risk of offending the French, should de Gaulle come to hear of it?

I was looking forward with professional interest to meeting Lord Louis's socialist adviser; he was at university with the admiral and had been politically influential to a marked degree.

Night had fallen on Singapore when I arrived at the Payar Lebar airfield. Captain the honourable James Gunn started his jeep and moved slowly from the control tower to the side of the aircraft. With me safely aboard, we made the journey back to headquarters in very quick time.

Lord Louis was attending to urgent after-dinner dispatches from London and various commanders scattered about South East Asia, when the small pilot light in the anteroom flashed red and went out. It was a full five seconds before the lamp glowed amber: this told the admiral that his private anteroom was occupied... by his "secrets" man and this remarkable fellow from Saigon.

He read again the signal from Gracey and pressed a button under the shade of a small lamp. He held it until a click told him the door of the private anteroom had opened. Gunn had seen the green light, his signal to enter the Supreme Allied Commander's office, without being seen by other headquarters' staff.

The large double doors on the far side of this splendid room were closing behind the departing WRN officer-secretary as Gunn and I emerged from behind an ornate Chinese screen.

Lord Louis rose in welcome, inviting us to sit, while running an eye approvingly over his visitor. He tossed the signal over to me. "Well, colonel, what's it all about?"

I outlined the proposal, giving my own evaluation of each phase. I described the individuals, politicians and fighting men, both Chinese and Vietnamese. Lord Louis listened closely, his lively imagination responding. I paused for the admiral's reaction.

"He's right, of course, Chiang Kai-shek is an ally. Clever little man, isn't he?" said Lord Louis. "And what a neat proposal—though the idea of Chiang aiding a communist sounds unreal somehow. But I get the point about the Chinese wanting to help their ex-patriots. What isn't so clear to me is—what's in it for Chiang?"

"With nothing to prove it," I told Lord Louis, "I believe Chiang is arranging his comfortable future as part of a well-staged handover to Mao and his communists."

"You're not serious?" said Lord Louis in disbelief.

I'd been working on a hunch based on unconfirmed reports that Chiang and Mao had done a deal. Professor Lien indicated this when he said Chiang's regime would be gone in a few years' time.

"He's not going to win against Mao politically or militarily, and he's smart enough—or perhaps it's Madame Chiang—to know it." I explained further: "Such an arrangement is in character with the Oriental, they never fight the inevitable when a suitable alternative will suffice."

"What is meant by 'his comfortable future'?" asked Lord Louis. "You mean some sort of partitioning deal?"

"Something of that sort, but not on the mainland. Probably one of the large islands offshore, like Formosa."

"Since there's a grave risk of civil war, and all the attendant misery and suffering it brings," said Mountbatten, "I'm willing to proceed toward a suitable arrangement. But we can't set up a meeting until I've cleared it with the PM. And what about the French and Americans?"

"Can I go on negotiating time and place, subject to London's approval?" I asked. "No need to involve the French or Americans at this stage; let's play it by ear."

Mountbatten was silent, deep in thought. "Yes." He then nodded his head in agreement and warned, "But be careful, colonel. Forgive me if I seem to doubt, but any leakage— if any whisper of this gets out—we've got the biggest international headache known to contemporary history. This whole thing must be conducted in absolute secrecy."

I smiled at him reassuringly; no word was spoken, nor was necessary as Lord Louis continued, apologetically, "I should have known better, forgive me. How about a drink? I've asked a few of my staff to come and meet you, to exchange ideas. I propose that we write an intelligence appreciation covering all aspects of political, military and, with the help of experts, economic and social future of South East Asia, projected over a specific period to be agreed upon."

Lord Louis introduced me to each of the dozen or so officers from all three services, and instructed Gunn to brief me as to the specialities of individuals. All were on my list with one exception; I found no difficulty in picking her out. She was the only woman there, until later, when Lady Louis joined us.

Intelligence officer Natalie Fitzgibbons, WRNS, was no more than twenty-six, about five feet seven and beautifully proportioned. It was her eyes of deep amber pools with glints of green that flashed signals, and though no beauty in the classical sense, the overall vision was exceedingly attractive. I was aware of her physically as Gunn introduced us. Almost immediately I tuned into her intellectually as words were exchanged.

Gunn explained in detail the special undercover assignment of Natalie and, as if by design, left us alone. I wondered about this, so naturally expected something unusual to develop. I was not to be disappointed.

"Don't let's talk too much shop, colonel. I'd much rather hear about life in Saigon and your personal experiences, which I gather are both exciting and satisfying. Business can come later." She paused, taking a brandy from the tray. "We've adjoining bedrooms, so with your permission I'd like to pay you a visit before you turn in, to explain the highly secret nature of my assignment. Even Captain Gunn doesn't know of it."

Long ago I had ceased being surprised either by people or events; since my work employed every artifice, both for survival and success, nothing was ruled out. But inside me, my pulse was running faster.

We talked for a while and, cautious as always, I told only of general conditions, making no mention of the real work I was doing.

"Ooh yes, colonel," her eyes trying to penetrate my mask, "but what's it *really* like? You must be steeped in problems of every kind. You haven't come to Singapore just to chat about the proposed grand intelligence appreciation, have you? Not when you're up to your ears in important work in Indo-China!"

Before I could reply, and I was glad of it, Lord Louis re-joined us, and, after mildly reproving Natalie for monopolising me, took me away to meet a group of officers—he'd decided time was too limited for individual discussions.

"You come too, Natalie," he added. "We want your views."

It was midnight when I answered a light tap on my door and Natalie, almost unrecognisable out of uniform, came in.

She left me after a couple of Priapic hours and I must confess to being amazed that she could outstrip me both in passion and audacity; this was a new, pleasant experience.

Natalie Fitzgibbons's secret assignment, it transpired, was a conspiracy between her and Lady Louis Mountbatten to seduce me. It seems my reputation with Saigon ladies had made me a special attraction! I laughed at myself, having never given it a thought that SAC would unwittingly provide such excellent companionship. I would reciprocate, if given the opportunity.

My departure the next day was most circumspect. Lord and Lady Louis saw me off, with Gunn driving the jeep.

The smile on Lady Louis's face was, I thought, a shade naughty, but discreet—the kind that has an unspoken message.

A last wave. We slowed at the main road and turned right for the airport. Lord Louis had sent off his message to the Prime Minister; it was now waiting time, but I was to carry on with arrangements.

Gunn swung the wheel to turn in through the airport gate, up to the control tower and report arrival. He had telephoned earlier—with luck the plane would be ready. On the way we'd discussed the visit and the proposed meeting between Lord Louis and Ho Chi-minh. Gunn, wanting to clarify a point, asked, "How did you get on with Natalie? Damned nice girl, don't you agree? And very smart. All there, that one!"

I'd wondered when this would come. I wondered, too, if Gunn suspected that Natalie had entered upon her own secret assignment. Or perhaps he'd had a hand in it!

"We got on very well. As you say, she's clever. Yes, we have a lot in common," I replied, as the jeep rode on to the tarmac to approach the plane.

Engines were turning but, not yet synchronised, were too noisy for easy conversation; I shouted a last farewell and "Thanks for everything" and leapt from the jeep.

Gunn watched my plane climb into the evening sky, possibly thinking: "Andrew Grant's one hell of a guy, brimming over with confidence—the arrogant *******!"

12

ALL THOSE INTERESTED in making things happen in Saigon had been hard at work while I was away in Singapore. Of these, none was more active than the Russian Boris Ulowski. He had a way of making something out of that which others failed to find interesting or useful. Probably this was because he had animal instincts, being closer to the wild than ordinary humans. He belonged to a special branch of Russian Counter Intelligence, a development of OGPU, their sinister secret police. Young for his rank of colonel, he was being groomed for big things.

It was Ulowski who, through his special skills, produced information that led to the execution of a very senior Russian official caught spying for a foreign power. This brought him promotion and favour with those able to further his professional ambitions.

Developed to a fine art, his powers of what he called "observation and relativity" possessed an uncanny ability to relate behaviour to intent with deadly accuracy. His Far East division of watchers, comprising both men and women with highly developed senses, trained by Ulowski in his special techniques, was capable of such fine judgement as to be able to determine an outcome from patterns of behaviour, with remarkable success.

These watchers logged every journey made by a chosen suspect, and every person contacted; even every building visited. While unusual changes in behaviour patterns were given special attention, names and ranks of those encountered were logged for further research. These in turn would be watched and assessed. From all this Ulowski deduced aims and objectives, then passed the information to others for action.

The agent he'd assigned to me found things difficult. Ulowski went berserk when told I was missing; though, knowing my reputation for cunning, he should have expected it. Time was spent learning I had gone to Hanoi. Ulowski now had something else to assess. Baffled, he fretted over it, searching for reasons and clues, without success.

Ulowski had watchers on everyone of importance among the British, Americans, Chinese, Vietnamese and French officials. My trip remained a mystery—which made Ulowski very angry, I was told by those watching him.

He had no such problems observing Professor Lien, who showed contempt for those tailing him; so sure was he of Ho Chi-minh's power and ultimate success, he could flout Ulowski.

An agent assigned to watch Lien witnessed the two visits to Hunter's HQ and my arrival on each occasion. After the first visit, Ulowski increased the watch on Lien. The payoff came when, to his absolute delight, he personally observed from the next-door rooftop the meeting of Lien with Ho Chi-minh, Mao Tse-tung and Lin Shao-chi, at the Sun Wah Restaurant in Cholon, a suburb of Saigon where Chinese merchants lived.

Ulowski must have decided these two happenings were in some way related. Because Lien was in both events he knew there was a connection, his intuition told him so. Most likely it was the burning of the paper on my second visit that seemed to confirm this.

Following Lien to Hunter's place for the third time, he was spotted as he manoeuvred himself into position so as to see into the office, hoping to find the vital all-confirming clue, only to be disappointed and further confused when I failed to appear. I'd changed tactics since Suzie's warning of French interest in Lien—I'd decided against personal meetings, leaving Hunter to act as go-between.

Ulowski knew that Ho and the French no longer met secretly, and that Ho had stopped talking to the Russians: he would know this too. He would have reckoned that Lien held the clue to some deal being rigged with the Chinese, and decided I'd got something to do with it.

All recent happenings, including my trip to Singapore, plus the Sun Wah meetings, were related—Ulowski would be sure. Only my visit to Hanoi puzzled him. Why had I gone as a brigadier? Must have visited someone of great importance! Who? And why at this time?

The date of the Japanese surrender parade in Saigon had to be advanced to dovetail with Lord Louis's arrival in Siem Riap. Revisions to plans and programme became necessary.

Word was eagerly awaited from London confirming the meeting with Ho Chi-minh, so that finer points of detail might be applied without last-minute risky adjustments.

The ailing Field Marshal Count Terauchi, Commander of Japanese Forces in South East Asia, was ordered to have his troops ready by that date and work was accelerated to have the spectator stand of 1,000 capacity ready in time.

French colonial police reporting to me stated their drive against communist undercover agents—who were spreading rumours to frustrate efforts to restore effective government—had been of limited success.

British Military Police reported that grading the Japanese war criminals into "blacks, greys and whites" was proceeding slowly due to reluctance of witnesses to come forward. It was hoped to devise ways of improving things, even to the extent of offering inducements.

I blew my top at this. "For Christ's sake, *now* is their chance to *get even*—and they need *inducing* to do it?!"

In other areas things were inexorably moving on. Evidence of France assuming administrative responsibility was plain to see, making the likelihood of internal war more frighteningly imminent.

Why the haste, I wondered. Maybe Peter Bain would know. That Gracey had a cosy relationship with Le Clere was evident... the dinner parties for one thing; their frequency and the choice of guests, mostly French senior civil servants, were further signs. If only London would approve this meeting between Mountbatten and Ho... some miracle might still save the tragedy that loomed closer and closer as the minutes passed.

Admiral d'Argenlieu's arrival, carrying out de Gaulle's instructions, made a great impression on French colonialists, reassuring them de Gaulle would restore Indo-China to its former glory. Established in the Palais de Cochin-Chine, and very much de Gaulle's man, he was set on becoming the first post-war governor of this French colony.

This strange man: d'Argenlieu was French High Commissioner to Indo-China as late as 1946 as a Carmelite monk missionary, having left the navy to become a priest. French navy officers had governed Indo-China during the final decades of the nineteenth century in close alliance with the Church. Admiral George Thierry d'Argenlieu did something odd when World War II broke out: he re-joined the French navy, discarding his cassock for a uniform.

Now, his first act is to rename one of Saigon's main thoroughfares Rue General de Gaulle— to the delight of some and disapproval of many, particularly those with nationalist leanings, supporting independence for Vietnam.

D'Argenlieu was incensed over the intransigence of Ho Chi-minh. Before leaving France he had been assured that Ho, though a tough negotiator, would talk. To find him unwilling to keep to the agreed procedure for discussions was infuriating and embarrassing: more than a proud Frenchman could stand!

Blame for this automatically fell upon both Russia and China, but as no evidence supporting these suspicions had been produced, no official action was possible. All this created a frustrated and angry admiral.

Suzie Barbancourt described to me how he, in his late sixties, maybe early seventies, took her hand, raising it to his lips, asked impatiently to know if she'd "got started yet". He wanted to hear some good progress report about Ho Chi-minh.

Suzie told him she'd done the preliminaries and the real work began as of now. She'd met Major-General Gracey and Lieutenant-Colonel Grant, and didn't anticipate any problems.

The admiral asked if any rumours were in circulation.

She replied evasively, "Nothing worth telling." But she hoped to have "something on Ho Chi-minh very soon". She was deliberately cautious, she told me, so as not to be forced into revealing too much too soon. She was also waiting for news promised by me.

Suzie was relieved when the admiral, realising there was nothing to be gained by further questions, let her go to get on with the job.

It was at our daily meeting Suzie told me of these events. The admiral, she said, was disappointed. He'd expected a better report from her. He was morose and showed it.

Suzie told me she left feeling she'd cheated him—but in a good cause.

Upon leaving the admiral, she'd made straight for her contact, a rendezvous arranged at an apartment in the Rue Catinat, the abode of a friend who was still in Paris. She was apprehensive as to the outcome because her previous association with this particular contact had been awkward and unhappy.

Suzie had found him—Chief Superintendent Deshampneuf—already arrived. As always, he was out of uniform. Because the nature of the assignment required it, his mood was ugly: special covert operations like this always worried him. Working again with Suzie was not of his choosing; he feared that, as before, it would be an unhappy relationship. Suzie, too, was uncomfortable. She said he seemed to shiver as he attempted to recall happier, more intimate times during Resistance days, and the souring of their relationship for reasons he will have wanted to forget. Knowing him so well, she pictured him wondering what this reunion would bring; Suzie, too, had wondered about her reaction when on opening the door they were to come face to face.

As she looked him up and down she saw a difference; he was fatter. She teased him about it, but liked the beard and told him so. She remembered his tame reply, spoken as much in appeal as greeting.

"Hallo, Suzie" was pathetic, weak.

Her answer, "Hallo, Jacques," was not affectionate, more in pity, as she'd kissed him lightly on the mouth.

She was surprised when Jacques smiled and responded with an equally light, meaningless, mouth-to-mouth touch, raising his eyebrows as he stepped back.

Anxiety made him jittery, as too much was going wrong for the French in what should be their backyard. As usual, he would be heavily dependent, Suzie knew. He would expect her to make the first opening in the veil shrouding the mystery; he was never a leader.

Suzie found his demands irksome: he wanted to know how far she'd got, and what she made of things. His tone revealed his desperation. She had to calm him, stressing the need to keep a clear head. She said she wasn't sure, but almost certain, I was involved in everything that was going on; that I'd got the whole scene covered with experts, and nothing could happen without me knowing about it.

Deshampneuf demanded to know if she planned to work with me. Suzie explained I'd already agreed to work with her on the leak, and the Ho silence.

The superintendent asked why, in disbelief, with a tone of fear.

Suzie told him it was the best way of finding out what

I was up to. We'd combine this with vigilance. She insisted that he put his best men to watch me, night and day, if they were to learn a lot from my contacts.

The superintendent doesn't think this possible; he's approached the good agents he had pre-war and they're either working for that "Dutch bastard Blitz" (who works for me) or for the "bloody Americans".

Suzie asked if they will double.

He thinks there's no chance, they're scared to death of being found out. He'd already tried this and they'd told him they wouldn't live five seconds if I or the Americans even suspected them.

Suzie told him she's puzzled about me, and can't see what the British have to gain by interfering. There are times when she doubts her own instinct about me being involved—she feels there's a hidden factor somewhere.

She tells me of her surprise when the superintendent opened the door in answer to a coded rat-a-tat and introduced the diminutive Nuyen-dinh, to her astonishment. She'd never seen a real dwarf before.

Deshampneuf told her not to be fooled by his size and explained that looking like a child added to his value; nobody expects a boy to be a secret agent.

Suzie had spoken in Annamese, but was answered in purest French, the diminutive man explaining that he'd been working on a tip about a Professor Lien. He'd then reminded Deshampneuf that Professor Lien had been associated with Aubaire before the war in Hanoi.

Deshampneuf nodded. Suzie was surprised to hear Nuyen-dinh say that Lien had been seen in Saigon. Lien, it seemed, had contacts connected with Mao Tse-tung and had been making visits to British Security HQ near the cathedral. He'd been there twice, and once a British colonel had arrived. This had got to be important in some way, Suzie had agreed (realising it must be me). They thought this might be the break they were looking for. If Ho was up to something with someone other than them, it had got to be the Russians or the Chinese.

But why Mao Tse-tung? who they knew had no power base. None of the Allies would go along with that. Deshampneuf was mystified.

At the time, Suzie was also baffled, and reminded Deshampneuf of that hidden factor she'd told him about. She suggested he put Nuyen-dinh onto watching me.

13

I WENT TO the airport to greet Captain Gunn on his arrival in Saigon. The Prime Minister had left Lord Louis to decide, based on local intelligence, if it was not too risky to proceed with the Siem Riap meeting. In any event, it was to be purely exploratory as a possible way of averting the threat of civil war.

"So you're to announce SAC's visit to Angkor Wat to the press?" asked Peter Bain. "Is this wise?"

"No good hiding it," replied Gunn. "A private visit to the ruins is harmless, and natural enough. Lord Louis is just taking a break."

The general agreed, adding, "Incidentally, Field Marshal Terauchi has pleaded to be excused attending the surrender parade on health grounds."

"Has our doctor seen him?" asked Gunn.

"Yes. And he confirms him weak after his recent stroke. I think he wants to be spared the disgrace of appearing before the news cameras and the public."

"He asks for a private ceremony," added Bain, the diplomat, with a touch of sympathy for the old man.

"Lord Louis might prefer this," said Gunn thoughtfully.

"I'll ask him, if you have no objection, sir, or would you prefer to handle it?"

"Please do," the general answered. "It might be best that way [thinking of himself in a similar situation]."

Gunn and I got together over the special security aspects of the secret operation at Siem Riap.

"There are many wrinkles still to be ironed out," I explained, "but I hope to have a final plan for the meeting on the day of the surrender."

"That's time enough," agreed Gunn. "Do you think the Americans, French or Russians have any inkling of what's going on?"

"I don't think so; they are suspicious but I see no reason why they should have worked it out."

Gunn pondered this, pulling on his cheroot and inhaling deeply. "Even if they have, there's no likelihood of any fireworks." Pausing, he added apprehensively, "Is there? SAC's not at risk, is he?"

"I've thought about this a lot. It's hard to say. The French are worried sick that Ho has stopped talking to them, so they'll suspect something. These observations I mentioned will tell me what all principals have been up to for the past week. We've had tails on all of them including this Captain Barbancourt. Deshampneuf, the new head of Sureté, aroused my interest when he obliquely suggested I had killed Aubaire, his predecessor. If he hadn't, I would have left him out of the reckoning but it seems he and Suzie Barbancourt have something going—and I don't think it's a love affair. Barbancourt is something special, I'm sure. Deshampneuf may also be. I think the French, more than anyone else, would do almost anything to stop this meeting. But I'm certain they don't know of it, nor do the Russians. I suspect they are watching me too, but I've taken care of this."

Through a cloud of smoke, Gunn said, "For Christ's sake, keep it that way until it's all over." As an afterthought he asked lightly, out of the corner of his mouth, "And *did* you kill Aubaire?"

I simply winked above a subtle smile.

"Remember, Andrew, if there's the slightest chance of danger the Prime Minister has ordered immediate cancellation. You understand this?"

I nodded.

After Admiral d'Argenlieu's official reception, I went back to my apartment wondering why Suzie hadn't been at the party. My thoughts moved to ways of getting the message to Lien. Both Field Security HQs were being watched. Two tails were on me and it was inconceivable that Blitz, Sieling and Maryse would be neglected. In the business of intrigue nobody who hoped to succeed in finding out what I was up to would fail to watch my most astute, ruthless and dedicated threesome. With this in mind I decided to ignore the watchers and be simple and bold.

I told Hunter to send a verbal message to Lien, using one of his drivers: "They can't watch everybody, and a plain-clothed corporal won't attract attention. Even if it did, its importance would seem minimal."

I poured myself a nightcap and sat writing a situation report for the weekly meeting Peter Bain was chairing tomorrow. My contribution covered political security with a military flavour, whereas that of Bain dealt solely with diplomatic activities and considerations of civilian concern.

Answering a rap on the door I came face to face with an artist-like version of Suzie. I had mixed feelings about her.

She moved lazily forward. I felt her arms go around my neck, she kissed me passionately while her body moved against mine.

I was content to forget work. The physical has demands too. All the more so, when a lovely from Haiti is unbuttoning your clothes and making sensual sounds between French kisses. My surrender was total, as was her victory.

We wakened to the dawn's command. Its brilliant light crept rapidly across the rooftops and splashed into the room. I looked at the time, smacked Suzie lightly on her bare bottom, and told her to wake up.

"I am," she said sleepily.

I got up, threw on a silk robe and put a flame under the coffee pot. We both had a busy day ahead, but there was need to talk.

"Why weren't you at d'Argenlieu's last night?" I called from the bathroom.

"Had work to do," a sleepy voice replied.

"Sounds important. Was it successful?"

"No. I thought I had something good going with the wife of Pierre Bastien, who sits on the Joint Council. As so often happens when a prominent man is being lustful outside marriage, tongues wag and ideas of blackmail develop. Madame Bastien knows—but seems not to be concerned because she has a satisfactory affair going with one of your senior officers—a Captain Hunter, I'm told."

Now wide awake and sitting up, naked, she smiled at me coldly. She continued in that low melodious voice: "Captain Hunter is investigating the leak at the Joint Council, isn't he, Andrew? Why didn't you tell me?"

Displeasure lay behind her outward calm. She had reason, for I had intentionally deceived her and she knew it, no matter what I would say.

"I've hardly had a chance to tell you, things have happened so rapidly. It was on the spur of the moment I asked Paul to put out his feelers. I thought it might help. It's the way I work."

The cold stare remained and, measuring her words, she asked sardonically, "Who do you think would put a tail on me? I get the strongest feeling I'm being watched all the time."

"Almost every able-bodied man," was my smiling reply. "I don't think it strange in the circumstances." I wondered if Benoit was losing his touch. To disarm, I added, "I'm being watched too. It's part of the job. You should know this."

"But why me?" she pressed. "I'm only doing my job. I've nothing..." she paused, "...you mean because of the leak, is that it? That suggests something sinister, like a conspiracy against a legitimate enquiry into perfidy. And that means I'm dealing with nasty people who will go to any length to stop me finding out."

"Of course, you don't think—clever as you are—that your prying into this affair will go unnoticed. You'll be watched by the guilty to see how close you're getting. In my case there will be more than one wanting to know what I'm up to: for example, the Russians, Chinese, French and the Americans, all want to know as much as possible in this strategically important and politically fragile country. But, you know, they're wasting their time with me. I've nothing to interest them," I lied.

Satisfied this exchange had served its purpose, Suzie backed off. "Oh well, I'll just have to be more careful in future. I'll enjoy working with Captain Hunter, if that's OK with you?"

"Sure, that's fine. On the other thing—Ho not talking to you—we'll work together. I may have something good in a day or two. Meanwhile, it's best for you to go your own way, but stay close."

"How close?" she asked, reaching into my gaping dressing gown and squeezing hard, letting her nails lightly dig in. Lapsing into the foulest French, I fell on top of her. My thoughts went unspoken as she cradled me.

The crashing coffee-pot lid brought me, reluctantly, from the bed and I swore as the bubbling, steaming cauldron discharged its contents over the stove.

We were strangely happy over coffee and toast. A new kind of relationship had arrived. Something more than sex, but as yet unlabelled.

We made a date for tonight.

14

PROFESSOR LIEN HAD a date with Ho Chi-minh at the Sun Wah Restaurant, but he was not happy about the warning I passed to him of being watched by the French. If this was so, he figured others might do the same; the Russians, for example, and, who knows, the Americans too! He was an academic, not yet accustomed to the role he was playing. He was worried.

The Sun Wah had two entrances, back and front: one for the staff and the other for customers. He decided to use the back one, in disguise. In suitable dress, he made his way through the dark streets to the wide road that had to be crossed without cover of any kind. He waited in the shadows of buildings until a group of people came by, and joined them as they crossed the road.

Suddenly the group dispersed at the corner of the street leaving him alone—for one fatal moment exposed to whoever may be watching. He was nervous and it showed in his hesitant behaviour.

This was enough for the watching eyes of Boris Ulowski who, through study of the minutest detail of a subject could detect any characteristic that, like fingerprints, positively identifies. Lien always dragged his left foot when turning to the right, the result of an injury long ago.

In haste, Lien made for the back door, by now his pulse racing, realising things might have gone wrong. The very thing he'd worked to avert had happened; he must have been seen, he thought in alarm. He was worried. He thought he'd got this panic under control, so sure was he of ultimate victory by Ho Chi-minh.

Apprehensively, he lost no time in getting to the top floor and along the passage to the room where he revealed his fears to Ho Chi-minh.

Ho will have told him not to worry. Ice-cool Ho has reasoned that these people can learn nothing by watching Lien. They won't know whom he meets or, even if they do, it tells them nothing. He has nothing to worry about, Ho will assure him.

In calmer mood Lien relates his report, telling that Mountbatten, his wife, his daughter and aide-de-camp (ADC) will be in Siem Riap for the nights of 27th and 28th September, leaving on 29th. Lien explained that a method of contact has to be arranged as soon as he arrives at the Grand Hotel.

Ho wanted to know if this fits in with our plan.

Lien confirmed that it will, and the details will be conveyed to me on the morning of the 26th when I arrive at Siem Riap. Lien explained I am travelling by road with guard troops and a Signals unit to keep the admiral in touch with his Singapore HQ.

Ho smiled, happy that it allows plenty of time, his head nodding as if to confirm that, for this moment anyway, he could hope for—rather than merely dream of—independence.

I studied the list Eddie Blitz gave me and was surprised to see Marie-Claire Simone's name as group leader of a section of the French Youth Committee for the Restoration of Colonial Status for French Indo-China. This was now a matter for further investigation, I decided. Despite earlier assurances from the good doctor that his daughter would never become militant, Eddie's report suggests otherwise.

Hunter's and May's ex-MI5 experts had also done their stuff, producing reports that were very informative. Having been supplemented by Military Intelligence (MI) in London, two names stood out as most dangerous: a man and a woman. Both French civil servants and members of their university communist parties, according to French reports from Paris and Rouen. By political design, both had avoided being associated with Vichy French or other extremists during the war, to be eligible for suitable government employment in sensitive areas. Conveniently, they subsequently resigned party membership, but remained anti-establishment. Both were sex deviants who became Marxists, the man eventually adopting the more pernicious form of Trotskyism. They met for the first time when directed to apply for civil service appointments in Indo-China; things developed from there.

Most alarming was the knowledge that these two now occupied extremely sensitive positions in which they would handle top-secret information. The man, secretary to the Joint Council; the woman in the position of senior private secretary to General Le Clere.

Hunter's description of the man's social life made him the perfect target for blackmail. The woman, on the other hand, had no obvious blemish. She was clever: her lesbian pursuits were confined to her sister, a widow. Their camouflage was to have occasional sex with some man or other, thereby appearing heterosexual.

This was just the kind of information I wanted for Suzie. The question was, whether to broach the other matter about Ho Chi-minh at the same time. I decided not to.

With only five days to go to the surrender parade, much remained to be done. It was important that I be uncluttered with detail. I decided to offload, and the man to carry the burden was Freddie Coombes, one of the general's brilliant young staff officers, clearly marked for military stardom.

I was arranging this when the chief of staff buzzed to discuss details of the Terauchi surrender. This was one thing I could not get rid of.

"Will you come yourself, Andrew? Or send a rep?"

"I'll be there," I replied, while making a note to ask the French for a situation report covering the notorious Plaine des Joncs as far as Phnom Penh—the route both Hunter and I would take to Siem Riap.

I hung up and was buzzed again on the direct line. Peter Bain was on the intercom, "Can I see you, Andrew?"

The next minute Bain came through the office door and excitedly handed me a long message. He eased into a chair at his side of the desk. "This makes pleasant reading. But not what I expected when you asked me to check on Suzie."

I read quickly, unable to hide my excitement at what I saw.

"I thought there was something of interest, but not this, Peter. You're clever sods to dig up this stuff. Suzie *is* something special. So, I see, is Deshampneuf. Both in the Maquis, and together most of the time. See this, Peter." I pointed to the paper, Bain nodded, puffing on a long cheroot. "'Double agent known to, and recognised by, both French and British Intelligence. French code name "Sabot" and British "Spitfire".' That fits. And, see here, she married an Englishman who died through official French 'negligence'. Wonder what that was?"

"Very interesting. But read on. Deshampneuf could be a threat if she's persuaded to our side in this business."

"Obviously reverted to her maiden name. Dear old Suzie—quite a gal—and all those unworn decorations. How do you read it, Peter? Is this a clearance to employ her if we can? Have you discussed this with the general?"

"Yes, very briefly; he's not sure, he wants to discuss this with you and told me of the doubts you had of her at your first meeting. I gather he's rather chirpy about it. You thought there was something sinister about her. Had quite a laugh at your expense."

I looked at my watch while recalling the moment, telling Bain the gist of the incident. We were both laughing as Bain rose to leave.

15

DESPERATION DROVE A frantic Deshampneuf to use his best agents on the case at the expense of other work. He was rewarded when a lucky contact produced a tip-off, which led him and Suzie to a bungalow where Ulowski was engaged in his special type of interrogation. Watching through a side window, they saw Ulowski get up from the table and make for the rear of the building along the passageway.

The pugnacious Russian inhaled deeply the aromatic smoke from the butt of a large cigar as he entered the back room. Deshampneuf and Suzie slipped silently into the building, in time to hear Ulowski speak.

"Any luck?" he asked of two powerful Vietnamese, stripped to their underpants; heat in the room was intense as the windows were shut to muffle the screams of their victim.

The big Vietnamese released Professor Lien's hair, by which he'd been pulling him around the room, and turned his perspiring face to Ulowski, swearing in the negative.

"Keep at it," ordered the Russian. "You get the information out of him or you've had it!"

Anxious to leave the scene and its foul, stifling heat, Ulowski slipped back through the doorway into the comparative comfort of the passage. He leant against the wall, inhaling the sweeter air and closed his eyes in relief, just as Deshampneuf, chopping into the carotid, silently administered the knockout.

Ulowski's knees gave way; the remains of the well-chewed cigar flew from his mouth; the superintendent lowered him to the floor gently and silently—unconscious.

Suzie was first through the door, her snub-nose automatic ready for instant use. The two surprised Vietnamese were confused for just a second or two, then did the silliest thing: they picked up the professor and, using him as a screen, advanced on Suzie. The superintendent, who was now by her side, moved to the other flank.

Taking them by surprise, Suzie and Deshampneuf advanced at speed, one on each side, a manoeuvre they'd perfected in the Resistance. Two shots, and a bullet ripped into each Vietnamite head, and the show was over.

Lien scrambled up, aghast at the speed of events, expecting to be shot any second. Suzie quickly comforted him, helping him from this hell hole with his memories of torture.

Deshampneuf was slapping the face of Ulowski to wake him. He came round. Lien, sore-headed but restored to relative calm, was able to walk with Suzie's help to the waiting police wagon outside.

Soon a befuddled Ulowski, firmly assisted by Chief Superintendent Deshampneuf, joined the party as they left for Sureté HQ.

Stafford May's men, tailing Suzie and Deshampneuf, had witnessed these happenings with Sie-ling, who left at speed to inform Hunter, who contacted me over the scrambler.

I smiled and listened. It was pure guerrilla stuff; basic training for house raids. I pictured the events as Paul described Suzie and Deshampneuf in action.

"It was the speed of things that impressed Sie-ling," said Hunter. "No doubt about those two, they're bloody marvellous, working in perfect harmony and precision."

I thanked him and set about evaluating the situation. As to the arrests, I was of two minds. How much would they reveal under French pressure? How much did Ulowski get out of Lien? I decided Lien would say nothing to anyone, even under torture. Ulowski could not have cracked him. I was amused that Ulowski had been put out of action so effectively, without May having to do it!

I must, however, secure the release of Lien, whose part in the meeting of Ho Chi-minh and Mountbatten could not be played by anyone else.

I pressed the intercom. It was time to report to the general and Peter Bain who, fortunately, were together when I went in.

"How does this help or hinder you with Suzie?" the general enquired. "Seems to me you've more to give her than she has to give you."

"The grey area is her feelings about her husband's death," I explained. "It could be awkward if she's loyal to de Gaulle. It all hangs on this, as I see it, the question being: does Suzie blame the French authorities for his death strongly enough for me to exploit it?"

Peter Bain, in pensive mood, was thinking back to when he, too, was thirty—he recalled a similar situation as First Secretary in Athens. The lady then to be persuaded about a diplomatic matter had liked him in bed, which made his official task easier. "There's an old, true saying, Andrew," he chuckled, "make her your mistress and you make her your slave! I offer this merely suggestively, you realise."

This produced a chorus of laughter.

"Well said!" from the general.

"I take the point. I'll see what can be done," I grinned, rising to leave.

"Keep us informed, Andrew," said the general.

"And be careful," warned Bain.

Suzie was not the same; I was not surprised. She had told me earlier that as she had re-tasted guerrilla action she would be a new person to me. And, for a whole heap of other factors, she would be easily elated or depressed, depending upon results. Several hours spent interrogating is tough enough, but when it is fruitless it is devastating, demoralising and exhausting, especially in a stifling jail.

This was how she looked, standing framed in the doorway of my apartment: her overall uniform stained with sweat; the jet-black hair, normally shining, was dull with dust. She carried her forage cap, moving with tired steps towards me.

"What the hell have you been up to?" I asked, surprised and shocked at her appearance.

"As if you didn't know," was spat out as she threw the forage cap at me.

I moved forward to comfort her.

"Leave me alone!" she demanded angrily.

"All right, I do know. So the sooner we talk, the better."

She flopped into a cane chair, its arms wide, with holes for a tumbler to rest in.

"What'll you drink?" I asked in soft intimate French. "Long or short?"

Her eyes were even darker than usual. She glared up at me, "Don't soft talk me, you two-faced bastard!"

This was the moment for showdown, I decided. "We're all the same in this business, aren't we, my darling? You're not exactly what you seem, are you? Miss Spitfire, or do you prefer Sabot?"

A total transformation, and she showed yet another personality. The tiredness was gone; replaced by a sense of the uncertain. She squirmed a little wondering where this was leading. What more did I know? A deep sigh and she said, "I'll have a very large Pernod on the rocks, then we'll talk."

I gave her the drink and watched her. The first big mouthful was what she needed. I saw its effect and handed her a lighted cigarette. She inhaled deeply, her eyes closed and her head lay back. The load was leaving her as the liquor and nicotine took out the tension.

"What's that?" she asked of the paper I held out to her.

"Read it and see."

"Clever Hunter," she said, reading and smiling for the first time. "Wonder how he found out about this—two spies inside our Joint Council and General Leclere's office?"

"I thought you'd like to deal with this by yourself, in your own way, so I've taken Hunter off the case. The field is yours, and it'll be a feather in your cap. Peter Bain got the gen from your embassy in London, and MI5 confirmed it."

"Thanks. Why so generous?"

"It's a French matter. It's best, diplomatically."

"Very clever." She paused. "Why did you call me Miss Spitfire?" Apprehension in every word—who could have told me about her activities in France with the Resistance? Nobody else knew her codenames.

"Peter Bain has the best connections." This was the critical moment. I continued with caution. "If I know that you were once a double agent, I also know that you and Deshampneuf were in the Maquis working for the Resistance during German occupation of Europe. Could I know that, without knowing that you were married to an Englishman who died through some sort of official French cock-up?" I paused, observing her reaction. "Want to tell me about it? Or perhaps it's a painful memory?"

For the first time, she spoke in French. It was the soft, tender kind, that is reserved for special things and children. "Yes, it's painful. I haven't thought about it for so long. I haven't wanted to. Poor Philip. He was so young and brave—foolishly so. He hated the Nazis so much he would undertake near-impossible missions to prove a point. How he survived so many, it's hard to know. It must have been the fierceness of his hatred that produced his cunning. One day he went to kill a Gestapo general visiting the area. Philip always worked alone. He was so excited, just like a kid on his first rabbit hunt, or a young buck on his maiden safari. They dumped his body in the village square with a note pinned to it, which read: 'Had he succeeded we would have kept him alive to suffer. But he failed so killed himself, as you all will do before long. Heil Hitler.' Someone betrayed him," she said bitterly, "but I never found out who it was."

She lifted the glass from the hole in the chair arm, looked at it, then at me. "Another," she asked, handing me the glass with its melted remains. No wet eyes, she was past this; but there was sadness, I could see. She must have loved him very deeply, I was thinking, while pouring Pernod onto ice cubes. Handing her the glass, I raised mine invitingly. "Here's to the future, chérie, may we find new happiness and new purpose together."

Her look was questioning. Her thoughts, almost loud enough to hear, brought a radiant smile. The big black eyes were dancing again, and colour tinted her dusky cheeks.

Later would do, I decided, to ask how official French negligence was to blame for Philip's death. If "someone betrayed him" it doesn't mean it had official blessing. Better to move away from this subject to more general things. "You said we'll talk. Did you have something special in mind?" This time she sipped the Pernod while stubbing out the cigarette as I lit her another.

"Yes, I'm making no real headway over Ho Chi-minh." The steel in her eyes appeared as she raised her head to look at me. "But I'm certain you could help me. Something inside me says you're up to something." A thin smile lightened her hard features as if inviting my trust.

"I take it you've had no joy with Professor Lien or Ulowski?" I used this to probe her sincerity. "But tell me, why did you arrest them?"

"I should think you could answer your own question," she snapped.

"Maybe, but it's important, if I'm to help you, to know your thinking—what led up to the arrest."

I could see Suzie was thinking hard. She decided to come out into the open to see what effect it had. "We've been watching Lien for days—and you, too," she began. "Both of you met on two occasions at Hunter's HQ. Lien came a third time but you didn't show. We figured that you expected to be watched so Hunter acted for you. Lien was visited by a man driving a British jeep, which was recognised as one of Captain Hunter's. The inference was simple, he was a messenger delivering your communication. Then out of the blue Lien was snatched by three men at an isolated spot near the airport. This led us to the bungalow where they sweated him. We allowed this to go on hoping Lien would break. We might then have more of his secrets to work on by grilling Ulowski. It didn't work out, so before too much damage was done to Lien we swooped to do things our way. And that's it. Ulowski has learned nothing and Lien was unbreakable."

As I'd thought, Lien would die before talking. I decided to probe a bit more. "Have you any idea of de Gaulle's plans for the country's future?"

"Yes, he wants to restore it to colony status."

"And you agree with this?"

"Yes, of course. Why do you ask?"

"Thinking people don't believe it can be done in these circumstances."

"And you rate me a thinking person?" she asked with just a touch of flippancy.

"Yes, I would have said so. It's so obviously wrong, I would have said you'd see it that way," I retorted.

Her query, "What are these circumstances you mention?" changed the mood to serious.

"Begin with Ho himself," I reasoned. "He's committed to fighting for independence and has a formidable army in the field. Then there's his backer. At one time Mao Tse-tung, now so powerful that soon Chiang Kai-shek will be ousted. Should China fail, there's Russia. How d'you suppose France can win against these odds? Ho Chi-minh might get help from China and Russia, they both oppose the return of France as colonial master."

"How do you mean, win? You make it sound like another war. This time against our own people!"

This was pure colonialist reaction from one so far untouched by real communism and unaware of its appeal to the oppressed masses.

"I don't see it that way," she continued. "If Ho comes back to the discussions, de Gaulle is prepared to yield a little. But not over the south; this has to be ours."

"For how long?"

"I don't know! Who does!?" she replied with a touch of impatience.

"Think about it," I invited. "Even if you do a partition deal, Ho isn't going to honour it. He'll use every trick, dirty and otherwise, until he's ready to launch the inevitable major attack. When this happens will France have an army capable of countering him? You know this can't be."

"We're doing it in Algiers!"—a touch of pride in her voice.

"Just across the Mediterranean," I mocked. "Try sustaining a major war out here with China in the background supplying know-how and weapons! This will become a very bloody civil war. And think, my lovely, what happens to the Chinese population when Ho wins? His national purification policy must mean their departure, if not demise, not only on ethnic grounds but wealth and economics as well. Ho will want these things for his own people."

"Mon dieu, Andrew! Is it really like this? Are you saying we have to get out and leave everything to Ho? Maybe civil war will be averted but the Chinese problem remains?"

"Not necessarily. There are those who think Ho might be persuaded to a deal of independence for the whole country, with conditions. Among these would be the safeguarding of French and Chinese interests, including compensation for properties taken over in the national interest. There would be a Chinese Affairs Bureau manned by Britain and America to ensure adjustments in wealth transfers and resettlement in other countries willing to accept those desiring to leave the country. A time limit would be fixed when all foreign agencies would ultimately leave Indo-China."

"What makes these people think Ho will agree?"

"It's reckoned that he'll pay a price for immediate independence but, if made to fight for it, he'll take *all* as spoils of war. Allied governments, other than France and Russia, have indicated a desire to sound Ho out on this."

"Did France and Russia object?"

Now, I thought, comes the difficult moment. Her reaction to my reply was vital. I continued, "To be truthful, they haven't expressed an opinion yet. The agreed strategy is to meet with Ho first to get his reaction. If this is satisfactory, France and Russia can be told. If it's not, then Ho will be encouraged to return to the negotiating table and get the best deal going."

She pondered this, her eyes followed her flittering thoughts. "Yes, that's good," she decided. "In this way France has not been involved so can't be compromised. She's free to make the best deal she can. Clever about Russia, too. Now I see what you've been up to, chéri. But something's still missing. Something doesn't ring quite right."

"But how does it sound to you so far? Do you like it?" I pressed.

"To save the country from civil war, yes, I like it."

"Will you help me with it? We have to stage it here—it can't be done elsewhere. I'll tell you the plan, then the missing link later, but you realise it's dynamite in the wrong hands. Deshampneuf, for instance. What of him? How would he react? Can he be trusted to support us?"

"Not a chance! He's out! Fanatical patriot to the point of stupidity; no, not him! Let's see what it looks like with the missing link first before I commit myself."

We are both aware things between us have again changed. Our end-of-war, far-from-home tropical love affair was a convenience of pleasure without depth. Apart from the physical there had been nothing. Now we are getting close in a cause, as she had once been with Philip. She shuddered mentally at the void in her life that Deshampneuf had filled, out of loneliness and need.

"'The obvious often appears to offer more than mere substitute. It wears the deceptive mantle of virtue's providence, and fate is made to serve a purpose, not an ideal.'" A quote she recalled, which seemed to fit the case at a time when depression was at its worst.

I laid it out to her, explaining every detail of reason and decision. How the Prime Minister had authorised Lord Mountbatten to meet Ho Chi-minh unofficially in exploration of the possibilities—nothing more.

"The missing link," I explained, "is General Chiang Kai-shek. Ho has agreed to share responsibility for government with Chiang initially to ensure the well-being of the expatriate Chinese spread all over Vietnam. This was at the suggestion of Mao Tse-tung, of all people!"

"A communist with a capitalist!?" she said in disbelief.

"It's the only way, don't you see? Chiang is an ally of the Western powers whereas Mao Tse-tung is an unrecognised terrorist; we can't negotiate officially with him. Ho and Mao are satisfied with this arrangement as they are convinced Chiang's reign will not be for much longer. They, like us in the West—including France—don't want Russia's influence here and this is designed to keep her out."

"Very smart, but will it work?"

"Who knows? But we feel it's worth a try."

"There'll be hell to pay if de Gaulle finds out," she warned.

"The British Prime Minister thinks not, and is confident he can persuade de Gaulle because of other factors. The exercise is designed to test Ho's sincerity and this has long-term importance. He runs only a small risk in not telling de Gaulle at this stage."

"If it's good enough for Lord Louis, it's got to be good enough for me. Tell me more," she said with new eagerness.

I told her that Lord Louis's private visit to the Angkor Wat ruins was a smokescreen for the meeting with Ho. I did not tell her about it being held in the Grand Hotel, or when. This was typical, as I never tell all to anyone until I judge it right to do so. Until she was fully committed, it was certainly not right.

My plan to go to Siem Riap by road with guard troops and a Signals unit, through the guerrilla-infested Plaine des Joncs, caused her to ask with concern, "Isn't that dangerous? Why not fly up?"

"We've no plane big enough to carry the Signals vehicles. There are two: one two-tonner with the transmitters and receivers, and a very heavy trailer housing the generator. We have no option but the road. Want to come along? French troops report it safe."

She hesitated, "I'm just thinking. Sure I want to come. But what about Deshampneuf? This may be a problem. Also, I'm wondering how much the Russians have learnt through Ulowski's reports."

"I've thought about Deshampneuf. My idea was for us to suggest he comes along to advise on local security matters for Lord Louis's visit to the ruins. I'd like to have him where we can see him. As for the Russians, I don't think Ulowski knows much. He certainly hasn't got anything from Lien. The very purpose of the snatch was to learn something; he wouldn't have bothered if he already knew. No, Russia doesn't know! Of course, you'll detain Ulowski for the next few days, but Lien must be released because he has to tell me their plan for the meeting. And, of course, if he's in custody it will frighten them off. He's the link man."

Instinctively I felt she had been won over but, as always, I awaited a final, positive sign.

She looked at her watch and pointed to it so that I could see it was midnight. Stifling a yawn, her big dark eyes held me in deep searching scrutiny, and then produced the expression that revealed total capitulation.

"May I stay the night?" she asked, making it sound like a plea for something more than physical.

We spent the next evening discussing the situation. Suzie had problems. How to get Professor Lien released and what to tell Admiral d'Argenlieu. She had stalled twice already, pleading extreme circumstances prevented progress. She dug deep into her memory for anything she may have said earlier that he could pounce on. She decided it best to say her time had been fully taken up tracing the Joint Council leak, and gamble on the admiral being sufficiently pleased with the result to agree that more time for the other matter would be needed.

She had certain information to give him, but decided this was hardly likely to do more than frustrate him. Lien's arrest could not be mentioned as she intended it to be a non-event with his release. The arrest of Ulowski, on the other hand, was something else. Her mind examined the pros and cons for reasons why it should not be reported.

In her normal positive way she concluded that it would both please and satisfy the admiral to hear of Ulowski being connected with the two spies at the Joint Council: a simple stretching of the imagination in a good cause, she decided.

As for Lien, she would tell Deshampneuf the best way to find out what he was up to was to release and follow him.

To her surprise, Deshampneuf instantly agreed. No battle, no argument, not even a minuscule discussion. She became suspicious. Never before had he so easily accepted a suggestion of this importance.

"A brilliant idea, Suzie," with apparent sincerity. "Of course you're right. He's not going to talk so that's just what we'll do. Set Lien loose and follow him."

But she'd insisted, "Not Ulowski. We don't release him or he'll go for Lien again and spoil things for us. You do see that, don't you?"

Deshampneuf agreed to this—she had it made. Lien would lead them straight to Siem Riap.

Lien was set free next morning and went straight to a house on Rue General de Gaulle where he was to remain until someone came for him. I'd set this up in anticipation of his release.

16

THE CRITICAL MORNING arrives and I wait for Hunter to report. I check the time: almost 0400 hours and still dark. The eastern sky gives notice of dawn approaching as Hunter's jeep brakes outside Commission HQ. I run down the steps, calling "Morning, Paul," and pull myself in by the windscreen frame. "All set to go?" We're both excited that the show is starting. Hunter's party today and mine tomorrow.

Assembly point was the old barracks of the French garrison troops before the war, whose courtyard was still cobbled, odd and nostalgic to the British troops now billeted there. Hunter changed gear as he pulled on the steering wheel, turned into the yard and up the steep slope.

I ran an eye over the assembly of what looked like soldiers in jungle green. I smiled, knowing Maryse and Blitz were among them.

As we dismounted, the roar of an engine responding to a racing change announced the arrival of Stafford May, expertly bringing his jeep into line with the other vehicles. He leapt out, smiling infectiously, in time to join the others as they saluted.

"You noisy sod," said Hunter, good humour in every word.

"Just a show-off," I accused. "Morning, Stafford."

"Morning, sir," he said in his usual breezy way; the "sir" was to satisfy the moment of correctness on parade.

"At ease," I requested, moving to the line of "men". I sat on the bonnet of the first jeep and asked them to gather round. I spotted Maryse and wondered what she'd done with her shape. Flat-chested and slightly broad in the beam, she passed for a man on the short side. Hunter had made the slouch hat standard in his section and Maryse had lost her cascades of copper-coloured hair inside her hat. The sten slung over her shoulder seemed like it was in capable hands.

"You know the task," was my stock briefing opener. "What you don't know is this." I pointed to Stafford May's jeep. The camouflage netting in the back moved and flew over the side to reveal a Chinese man. "Come out, Sie-ling," I called. "Not perfect, but good enough to fool them in this light, and at a distance."

Sie-ling play-acted, emphasising Lien's notable idiosyncrasy of swinging his glasses, and they all enjoyed the joke.

"Sie-ling impersonates Professor Lien," I explained. "He is closely watched around the clock by successive native policemen in plain clothes. Captain Hunter knows them and the house on the Rue General de Gaulle. The plan is to supplant Professor Lien with Sie-ling and so deceive Deshampneuf and Barbancourt that Lien is still in the house. A diversion will be staged nearby and you will take appropriate action. There will be a lot of people on the street going to market, but you will stop all movement.

Sergeant-Major Dawney will decide the moment for Sie-ling to change places with Professor Lien, who will be wearing uniform and look like a Gurkha.

"Sergeants Fane and Grey, disguised as guerrillas, will start the shooting and pretend to be shot by us. You remove their bodies from the scene then re-open the road to normal traffic. The whole thing should be over in four minutes at the outside. By this time the sergeant-major will be on his way with Lien to the rendezvous point. And remember to use blanks—we don't want to kill ourselves! Nothing must upset the timing and nothing is to prevent us getting Professor Lien. Any questions?"

My gaze was towards Blitz who silently shook his head. Then to Maryse, who wrinkled her nose with a naughty smile.

"OK, lads, good hunting," I wished them. Then, mounting May's jeep, I said, "Until tomorrow, in Siem Riap."

The latest French situation report was on my desk when I returned to the office. I buzzed the clerk and went over the day's engagements. The last was most important, with Signals and Gurkhas in final arrangements for the movement by road of my troops and equipment, tomorrow.

A time had been set for the brigadier's meeting on Terauchi's surrender to fit in nicely after updating the general on arrangements.

"These came in late last night," said the clerk handing me three envelopes. I put them down as if playing patience, noting the tiny symbols that told me the author of each.

Opening Blitz's first, then Sie-ling's; both dealt with routine matters of communist activities. It was now clear that Eurasians were in a state of panic, the communists having worked on their fears of extermination purposely to cause havoc.

I had earlier decided on the southern route to Siem Riap, which the French considered reasonably safe. I saw no reason to change the plan. The distance was 500 kilometres whichever way we went.

Sergeant Fagge came through on the intercom. "The general's free now, sir."

"Did Hunter get away all right?" Gracey asked. "I heard the shooting, hope all went well."

"Perfect, we even had a couple of professional witnesses who gave graphic tales of two guerrillas shooting their way out of a house when Hunter's party was passing. They're two Foreign Legionnaires, who happened to be at the scene. Local people believe they were the guerrillas' target. The British soldiers were marvellous, they say! The 'guerrillas' were both 'killed', and carried away from the scene by the British!"

"Our boys must have been very convincing," said the general.

"And that will be helpful when Deshampneuf starts the inevitable enquiry. He's going to ask a lot of questions of the British troops and those two Foreign Legionnaires."

We both laughed at the thought of the superintendent trying to find Hunter, who would be in Siem Riap by tomorrow. And the two "guerrillas"—what happened to them?

"We won't disappoint him, will we, Andrew?" chuckled the general, knowing the plan.

"No, sir. Stafford May will cope very convincingly."

"How do you think of all these tricks, Andrew?"

"Comes naturally, sir."

"Of course. Your father's a barrister, I remember! That accounts for it." He obviously enjoyed saying this.

I gave him the programme for Lord Louis's visit to Siem Riap. "It's not quite complete because I won't know the actual time of the meeting until I get there. And, of course, I may not like their proposals. You see, I've arranged for the Royal Cambodian Dancers to perform at night on the temple terrace. They do this by flaming torchlight, so it has to be dark."

"Nice work. How was that arranged?"

"To be truthful with you, I had a feeler from Phnom Penh when the visit was announced in a news release. Gunn was here at the time, so I asked him to clear it with SAC. It's perfect camouflage, you see. A good reason for going to Siem Riap."

"Excellent! Perfect cover. All the breaks come to you. But, Andrew, you'll need all the luck you can get over this one. Your timing's so fine you've no room for error."

"It's tight, I agree, but there's really nothing to go wrong. Sie-ling, disguised as Lien, is appearing suitably at the window, also strolling in the garden, far enough away from his watchers to deceive them. May's man tells me that both Barbancourt and Deshampneuf have been on site and appear satisfied that Lien is still there."

"At what time does Sie-ling become a 'servant' and walk away from the house?"

"Our party goes through at 0500. He will have left four minutes before, ostensibly to go to market. At a predetermined spot, using cover of Dr Simone's garage, he will have removed the moustache and beard, slipped into the uniform concealed in his large shopping basket.

Without fuss, he naturally climbs aboard a jeep and becomes part of the scene."

"What'll be Suzie's reaction when she learns you've deceived her?"

"She won't know until much later. I've arranged for May to tell her, after we're safely away, that a change of plan was necessary and I want her in Siem Riap as soon as possible. May also has a copy of an original document naming Deshampneuf as the one who betrayed her husband. Peter Bain obtained it from his special sources. The last thing she'll do is betray me—she'll concentrate on two things: killing Deshampneuf without incriminating herself, and getting to Siem Riap. Benoit will be watching her all the time and will keep me informed by radio."

The general watched me closely as my plan unfolded. A slight chill disturbed the obvious grudging admiration and affection he had for me. This is the other me: ruthless in pursuit of the objective—the man he himself had approved for this difficult job. His own soldiers in the field had killed thousands in battle on his orders. He wondered where lay the difference between him and me. Surely, only in moment and method. Was he less determined, less ruthless?

I'd missed none of this, so fine is my keen sense of feel in the varied atmospheres of the mind. Subtle changes in a conversation's rhythm usually trigger the first alert, sharpening my senses to other successive signs. Eye and face muscle movements all read like the written word to those whose lives depend on this special kind of safety mechanism.

"Sounds cold-blooded, does it, sir?"

This shook the general, who had only paused in thought

for maybe two seconds. He must seem unmoved and just as tough as the young colonel in front of him.

"No! C'est la guerre, Andrew. To be honest," he lied, "I was having a flash of thought about Lord Louis in case somebody gets trigger-happy."

"Take it from me, sir," I said, giving him full marks for covering up, "this is not going to happen. If there's an attempt to stop the meeting and precautions prove inadequate, the target will be Ho."

"For God's sake! No! Andrew, this must not be."

"Don't worry. I know they've taken care of this. The man we'll see at the hotel et cetera will not be Ho. It'll be a perfect matching double: they have several. As one is killed or wounded, another takes his place. Ho himself will be disguised so as to enter without being noticed. Lien will tell me tomorrow how to recognise him."

"Thank God for that. Had me worried for a moment, Andrew. Diplomatically, HM Government could not be associated with Ho's murder. You see that? Even though he is a communist guerrilla."

The general was then able to answer himself on his earlier question. It seemed in some odd way a relief to realise that, whereas in war his soldiers killed anonymously, I killed each individual by precise design—merely a question of technique and purpose. Both the same in the end, he concluded.

17

IT HAD BEEN assumed that things would happen sooner, rather than later, when they released Lien. Now Suzie Barbancourt was uneasy that time was passing without Lien making any move. She had dashed to the house when told of the shooting incident, in case it somehow involved Lien. She thought of the possibility that it might be an attempt either to kill or kidnap him. Had it been his own people helping him to get away to Siem Riap, she reasoned, there would be no need for shooting.

The two policemen watching the house described the affair to her, confirming that Lien was not involved. She was relieved and stayed long enough to see for herself that he was still there—she saw him appear at intervals at the window, swinging his spectacles when not wearing them, as was his normal habit.

Satisfied, she hastened to the Sureté to inform Deshampneuf in case he had not heard of the affair; he had and was agitated. He had, in fact, been checking up without much success, which did not improve his irascible temper.

"I've been trying to locate a couple of Legionnaires who

witnessed the shooting and claim to be the target for the attack," he said sourly.

"Obviously you didn't find them," Suzie observed.

"No, but I will. Incredible that they were not hit at such close range. And there's no trace of the British troops who, witnesses say, killed the two guerrillas who started it all. They removed the bodies, it seems, but no one knows where they've taken them."

Anxious to calm him, Suzie told him she'd been there just a short while ago and saw Lien still in the house. "I saw him myself, so all is well."

"Moi aussi," he said in calmer mood. "Thank God for that."

Suzie told him she had to report to General Le Clere about the spy in his office. "So you'll know where to find me if Lien makes a move. I wouldn't be surprised if he goes tonight, under cover of dark."

"J'espère," said Deshampneuf, nervously. "I don't mind telling you, I'm feeling the strain. I need action."

"Hang on," Suzie said to encourage. "He'll go soon, I'm sure."

"Don't be away long," he called as she reached the door.

Sensing he was likely to break down while she was away, the only thing to do was to comfort him as she had many a time during the war. He was soon calmed and she left him in more placid mood.

Hunter's party made good time without incident as they passed through the village of Sadec. From there to Chandoc was regarded by a French patrol as a dicey area. Guerrillas had been reported stealing food and raping women. After a couple of miles Sie-ling, whose eyes were as those of the eagle, pointed over Hunter's shoulders across the dry rice fields.

"See to the left of the road by that lone tree? Something's moving. Looks like Vietcong. See the cap?"

All of 200 metres away, he could make out the distinctive four-pointed caps of Vietcong guerrillas. "There's another two. That's three. See them?"

The sun burned down, beating back off the road in a haze, blurring the approaching figures. Hunter, looking through his field glasses, ordered the driver to stop, while raising his arm in cavalry fashion to halt those behind.

"Yes, I see them. They're climbing the embankment to the road." He ordered: "Dismount! Prepare for an attack!" His troops debussed, each man taking as much cover from the vehicles as possible, while leaving a field of fire for their weapons. "Hold your fire!" Hunter ordered. "Must be bloody mad, three against us. Maybe they've got friends we can't see."

The guerrillas came on. Suddenly a burst of light-machine-gun fire came from the other side of the road. Hunter's first reaction was alarm, believing another guerrilla force was coming from their right. He shouted an order to the other vehicles to form laager from which to defend themselves. When he looked again to where the guerrillas had been, they lay in three twisted heaps, unmoving.

Two French soldiers climbed out of their foxholes, each covering the other's alternate advance until they reached the roadside. Cautiously they surveyed the area. One, moving in crouched position, climbed out of the dry paddy field and up the embankment. Peering over the top, and satisfied the guerrillas had no fight left in them, he moved towards the fallen men. Hunter's group could now see the head of the second soldier peeping cautiously up and down the road. They saw his weapon come to the ready to cover his companion's approach to the bodies. Suddenly, his gun roared into action, firing at the nearest guerrilla, who was pouring the contents of his magazine into the belly of the leading Frenchman taken by surprise, failing to anticipate that the guerrillas were lying possum.

Mad rage brought the second soldier onto the road, his automatic still belching non-stop into all the guerrillas. When his gun stopped firing, he cursed and cried. Falling to his knees, he cradled his now dead comrade in his arms.

Hunter mounted his jeep and, telling the others to cover him, moved forward, halting by the grieving soldier who wept, seemingly unaware of his presence. "Tough luck," said Hunter, in French. "Sorry your pal had to get it like that."

"Mon fils," sobbed the man in a Corsican dialect, "he was too eager, too keen."

Hunter could see the father was no more than thirty-five so the boy could have been a mere sixteen perhaps. "Did you know we were coming through?" he asked, to give the man something else to think about.

"Yes, captain. We had been told that three British jeeps would come through about now, today, and tomorrow a larger party. That's why we're here. We were told that an attack on both of your columns was planned. This is probably a reconnaissance party."

Hunter helped him to his feet and signalled to his men to come forward. They searched the guerrillas but found nothing of value, except the weapons. These were turned over to the French Company HQ to which the father and his dead son were taken. Hunter reported the event to the French commander, who acted quickly to ensure more troops would be positioned along the rest of the road to Siem Riap, and for tomorrow when I was travelling.

Weary and road-worn, Hunter's party eventually rolled into Siem Riap as the sun spoke its farewell in a glorious blaze of spectacular colour. The brilliant, dying salute to the day—emerald with gold splashing across the horizon as twilight clothed the sky—and night descended upon its own domain.

Making for the northern part of the town, where Maryse had a house they would use as Security HQ, the convoy entered the marketplace while trading was still in progress and the stalls ablaze with colourful lanterns. Chickens scattered, squawking, from their path. French soldiers strolled in search of pleasure, as pie dogs searched for scraps that fell from the cooks' tables as they trimmed the chickens.

Maryse gave directions as darkness rapidly fell upon the column. A track off to the right, over rough ground, led them to a two-storey wooden building of pleasing proportions and railed verandahs, which was most suitable for their purpose, as it stood alone in a clearing with no other house or building anywhere near.

Lights were on, and an old woman stood by the door as the column halted at the rear of the building. Maryse made a fuss of her and they went into the house, while the men did the unloading.

"We'll be staying for two days," Maryse told the old

woman, who was overjoyed to see her young missy again, after so long.

"What—all these men too?" she queried, with surprise.

"Yes, so get in plenty of food," Maryse replied, while hugging the old woman, whom she had not seen for three years.

❧

Paul Hunter appeared at that moment with Professor Lien, now out of uniform, looking for Blitz. Maryse said she had left him by the vehicles. She introduced Ba-ba, her old servant. Ba-ba liked the look of Hunter and told Maryse, in Vietnamese, that she wished she were younger, with this good-looker around. Maryse shrieked with laughter, knowing Hunter understood what she'd said. Hunter was amused and even Lien found a smile. Maryse explained this to Ba-ba, who ran off blushing, colliding with Eddie Blitz—to add to her confusion.

Light-heartedness gave way to the serious as Hunter detailed Sie-ling, who knew the area well, to take Professor Lien wherever he wanted to go.

Seeing that the house was rapidly converting into a workable HQ, Hunter left for the hotel to meet the manager and arrange rooms for Lord Louis and his party.

He selected, for its ideal position, one complete suite of six rooms, all with communicating doors, in a wing with a private entrance at the rear of the building.

18

FAR AWAY IN Saigon, Suzie and I spent an idyllic last night together before parting in the early morning for an unknown outcome of the next two historic days. Passion dominated, we devoured each other as if to make up for our last imperfect meeting and for reassurance that our relationship was worth preserving, come what may.

Aside from the limited satisfaction she drew from the arrest of the two spies and General Le Clere's praise and commendation, she felt inadequate knowing that Paul Hunter and I had really been responsible. She took comfort from our new relationship in serving a worthwhile cause together and reminded herself that she hadn't really come to stop the leak. It was the other thing that brought her to Saigon—the cooling off of Ho Chi-minh. She had been charged with finding out why. She now knew the reason but had elected to withhold it from the French and work instead with the British to promote peace—to prevent civil war. This made her feel better as she surrendered totally to my plan.

"Hey," she cooed, looking at the time, "you've a busy day, remember? It's four o'clock!"

I leapt out of bed and dashed towards the shower, changed my mind, came back and kissed her, cupping a breast at the same time. Over coffee and rolls we discussed our plans and agreed that Lien would most likely leave the house some time today.

"He'll make straight for Siem Riap," I said, "so be ready to leave as soon as you can, and contact me at the Grand Hotel."

"What shall we do with Ulowski?" Suzie asked.

"Let him go when we get back. Funny, isn't it, no one's complained about his detention? Wonder why!"

"Probably because they don't want, officially, to recognise him," she ventured. "Don't forget, he was knocking a Chinese communist about—they wouldn't want Mao to think this had their blessing."

"Clever girl," was said with deliberate emphasis to please. I wanted her to feel good about me; this was important for the next few hours.

I watched as she preened herself; in love with me, she whispered: "It's not just for this, but for wanting me and being so wonderful at taking me. I can still feel where you've been, and the thrill lingers."

Parting was swift. I leapt into the jeep, pushed the lever forward and roared away. She was to go straight to Sureté, where she now had an office. I rendezvoused with my party of Gurkhas and Signals, to head their departure to Siem Riap.

Lien's double is still in the house at four o'clock when Deshampneuf checks as the watch changes over. Sie-ling is playing his last act of deception convincingly.

At 0455 hours Sie-Ling, as a "Chinese servant" carrying a large raffia shopping bag, leaves the house as if on his way to market. This would be logged by the watching policeman who would fail to check back to see if this is a daily happening. Soon the "servant" is lost in the crowds going to market to buy or sell produce. At Dr Simone's house the "servant" turns in at the open gateway leading to the garage.

The crowds move, making way for my jeep leading the column. I look to the curb beside Dr Simone's house and see a "Gurkha soldier" emerge from the garage; he casually walks to the truck immediately behind my jeep and leaps aboard, blending into the scene—precisely according to plan.

19

PETE BENOIT CHANGED his disguise at least a dozen times since Suzie's remark to me about feeling followed. The chances were she still sensed being tailed. Benoit wanted to believe that his tactics were good enough not to be spotted but, even if his disguise was exposed, he could still do the job of keeping an eye on her—that's what I wanted.

From his vantage point in the little coffee bar he had seen Suzie enter the Sureté building and, as her old Citroën was in the street, it was reasonable to assume she was still there.

The fat Eurasian and his Vietnamese wife who run the bar stand idly chatting behind the counter when Stafford May enters and, making straight for Benoit's table, asks, "Bonjour, monsieur, permettre mois?"

Benoit, his long thin cheroot in one hand and a half-empty cup of lukewarm coffee on the table in front of him, was surprised and full of admiration for the change in May's appearance. Moustache and goatee beard did the trick.

"Certainment, asseyez-vous," replied Benoit.

"Café noir, s'il vous plaît," May called to the proprietor.

As the wife placed the coffee on the table and left, May,

seeming to be reading his newspaper, asked quietly in English, "Is she still there?"

Benoit nodded, tapping the ash from his cheroot into the uncleaned ashtray. May drank his coffee and left, paying the Eurasian as he went.

Inside the Sureté, May asked at the desk for Captain Barbancourt, giving his name as Monsieur Philippe Roman.

"One moment, please." The gendarme pressed a button.

After a while the bar-style, free-swinging doors clattered to and fro and a man he recognised as Chief Superintendent Deshampneuf emerged asking his business with the captain.

"It's purely personal," May told him forcefully.

Obviously impressed by May's elegant appearance the chief superintendent lamely invited, "Come this way," while wondering what this was all about. Escorting May through the swing doors and along a dismal corridor in need of soap-and-water treatment, nothing was said.

May was very concerned that visitors for Suzie were first referred to Deshampneuf.

Deshampneuf grew more suspicious and worried with each step as he hesitantly led the way along this narrow passage towards Suzie's office.

Her affair with me was driving Deshampneuf to insane jealousy. Stafford May's arrival added to his fears and he almost turned about at that moment to demand further information, but thought better of it and bottled it up. He was afraid at times that someone, somewhere would tell her of the part he'd played in her husband's death. Many times he wishfully told himself that this was impossible— still fear remained. Not wanting Suzie to know he had seen her visitor first, he stopped before reaching her office and simply pointed to the door.

May entered to Suzie's request, "Entre," and immediately decided that caution was required as the walls were simply wood-frame partitions, probably not soundproofed. He whispered in French and passed her a slip of paper with "Lieutenant-Colonel Grant" written on it. Suzie nodded her understanding, while saying formally, "Qu'est-ce-que c'est vous demande?" May explained loudly enough for his voice to penetrate the thin partition, that he was on a fact-finding mission and had promised mutual friends he would look her up.

May wrote while they talked. He turned the paper round for her to read: "*I have been asked to explain that, because of operational necessity, a change of plan was necessary. Andrew fears that you may feel cheated, so I'm here to explain.*"

He quietly told her of threats, probably by Ulowski's men, to kill Lien should he attempt to leave the house, and that I had devised a substitution.

"Lien is now in Siem Riap," he told her.

Suzie showed no sign of reaction. She simply looked hard into May's eyes. How to react was the problem. Did she call this man a liar? Had she not seen Lien for herself, yesterday? And Deshampneuf had seen him only this morning!

"I know what you're thinking," May said calmly, "but the man you saw yesterday evening and today was a plant; Lien left the house at the time of the shooting, which was staged especially for the purpose."

She could not resist a smile breaking through a mixture of thoughts, some angry, at being left out of it, but mostly of admiration for the man she now knew she loved. May saw the smile and felt better. It was an off-beat task, having to tell her—she was so feminine, so attractive. It was going to be even tougher giving her the document about Deshampneuf's part in her husband's death.

"Now I understand," she sighed. "Andrew really is a lovable bastard. And so clever. Have you noticed, he never tells some things? And when he does it's not the whole thing. You must be Stafford May. I've met Paul Hunter, and now you. What a trio."

May told her how Sio ling had walked away from the house disguised as a servant with a long thin false moustache; that he'd changed into Gurkha uniform carried in a shopping basket and joined our column that morning.

Suzie's laughter was all that Deshampneuf heard distinctly while straining his ears in the adjoining office.

"Mon dieu, quelle l'homme! Under our very noses," she said admiringly, in muted voice.

May put his finger to his mouth suggesting quiet while handing her the document. "This, I'm sorry to say, is sad and disturbing news, not only for you but to us, too. It's only because we believed you were in danger that the case was investigated. These are the findings."

She took the envelope and removed its contents, noting the official heading, OHMS. This sudden change of mood had set her internal furnace alight. She sweated, more from what she read than the humidity and poor ventilation.

Her hands gripped tighter on the paper and May knew she had reached the damning passages about Deshampneuf's betrayal of her husband. When she had finished reading, the paper fell from her hands like something unclean. Her shudder of revulsion transformed into hatred and her body stiffened, her fists clenched, and breathing became deeper; her nostrils spread in disgust and anger.

Finally, as though at peace, she relaxed, looking at May. "C'est mauvaise, I'm sorry you had to bring it to me—it couldn't have been pleasant for you. So you think he would do me harm?"

May knew of London's warning of danger should she work with us on the secret meeting, but said only, "He's been watched for some time. When you've been with Andrew he has gone berserk with jealousy. In certain places he's made threats against you. True, he's made them when drunk, but those who knew him pre-war say he is capable of murder. You, of all people, will know from Resistance days."

"Yes," she nodded, "I know."

"Because of this, Andrew put our best man to watch over you."

She smiled lamely, but still a smile. "Sur moi? I thought he was there to see what I got up to!"

May smiled, too, "Oh well, you know Andrew! But seriously, someone's there if you need help. It might be as well if you know what he looks like," he added, passing a photograph to her.

"I'm an old hand at this game. Disguise is my speciality—not many fool me. I suppose your man has used about ten or more methods so far! I'll wager that right now he's smoking a long thin cheroot with a half-full coffee cup in front of him by the window of the Green Parrot Café across the street. Right?"

Instinctively May hit the desk with the soft side of a fist to emphasise his whispered words: "You're all right, clever girl. But he's there should you need him."

"Thanks," she said. "Now, I've got a lot to think about. I suspect your visit will have to be explained."

A hell of a way to leave her but he knew this was how I wanted it.

On opening the door he continued speaking in French, and to give the impression he was recently arrived from France and returning there soon, he said, "I'll give your friends the message. I'll be in Paris in one week. Goodbye, Captain Barbancourt."

Deshampneuf waited. He heard the footsteps fade and went quickly into Suzie's office without knocking. "Nothing wrong I hope?" he enquired, with what sounded like worried concern.

"No." She replied calmly, knowing a whole succession of questions would follow. More had to be said so she decided to worry him. "This man brought news of Philip." She watched him change colour despite the heat: he paled first at the sides of the mouth down to the chin; then across the brow, which became a mass of sweat beads; the cheeks went grey, the eyes filled with fear.

Suzie had seen enough. "It seems there's an enquiry going on. Philip's father is a senior diplomat and has requested it."

Deshampneuf demanded to know who the visitor was and what kind of enquiry, but she was in no mood to talk.

"He's a government lawyer. Now I have things to do." Desperate to be rid of him she made to leave the office, for fear of a row developing.

"Where are you going?" he wanted to know, seeming to bar her way.

Her reason for leaving must now be one he dare not oppose, or try to prevent. Urgently she searched her mind; rapidly it came: "I have a date with Admiral d'Argenlieu." She left, thinking that at any time now Lien's departure must become evident. Those watching the house couldn't have seen a figure at the window for two hours.

She drove fast in the same Citroën I'd requisitioned for going after Colonel Drury; instead of turning left into the Palais de Cochin-Chine, she pulled the car's wheel to the right, taking the road to the airport. Approaching rough ground where stood the airport's tall sighting mast, Suzie looked behind her. Her constant companion was there, as she hoped, for now it was vital to use him in a scheme her mind was hatching.

Suzie pulled off the road behind thick scrub and got out. She smiled knowing that this unexpected move might put her shadow in a fix. Would he stop or go straight on? He had no option, she decided, since his sole responsibility was to watch her. But how would he deal with the unexpected this time?

To her pleasant surprise, he pulled off the road and stopped beside her, smiling. "Well, you wanna talk?"

Her reply was in Creole and his answer was the native dialect of Martinique. This started a congenial exchange resulting in Benoit suggesting a course of action for the disposal of Deshampneuf.

Suzie drove to the Rue General de Gaulle at speed. It was eight o'clock and the police watch was just changing. She asked the sergeant going off duty if all was well.

"Yes, madam," he replied, "no one's come out except the cook earlier."

"Has he returned?"

"Not yet."

"Have you logged this?"

"Yes, madam."

"Show me." She flipped over the page. "The cook did not go to market yesterday, according to this."

"No, madam. Maybe he goes every other day."

"When did you last see the professor?"

"Just before five o'clock, madam."

"That's three hours ago. Is this normal?"

"No, madam. He is usually seen more often at the window, and walking in the garden. Maybe he's unwell."

"Come with me, all of you," she ordered, and led them up the path to the front porch. Sending the two policemen to the rear, she threw open the front door and moved quickly through the house. It was empty—she knew it would be.

"Come," she ordered, and ran to the Citroën. The men piled in and she roared off, tyres screaming, heading for the Sureté.

Deshampneuf, already depressed, went berserk. It took a while for him to calm enough to listen. "Say that again?" he said.

She told him of her hunch that Lien must have been sprung during the shooting incident. "You said yourself it was odd that the Legionnaires were not hit at such close range. These British troops and the two guerrillas, where are they? It smells, I tell you, we've been duped. And I think I know who by."

"Who?" he demanded.

"Colonel bloody Grant, that's who! I'll lay you a bet he has Lien with him at Siem Riap. I believe that's where something's being arranged."

"What?" he asked desperately.

"I don't know what! But something to do with Ho's silence."

"But," he started, "we saw Lien at five o'clock this morning..." then finished sadly "...didn't we?"

"No, Jacques. My guess is we saw a plant who left the house this morning disguised as a cook going to market. Grant's column went through at the same time. Don't you see? We have to get to Siem Riap, quickly as possible."

She played the part well. Deshampneuf was convinced and they decided to leave at first light tomorrow.

20

ALMOST AT EXACTLY the same time as my party entered the southern outskirts of Phnom Penh, halfway to Siem Riap, Suzie and Deshampneuf were leaving behind the last native shacks of Saigon and entering open country— eager to reach the rubber estates, where trees provided shade.

Brilliant sunshine, already very hot, humidity almost unbearable, as a rain squall passed over them. Steam rose from the road, making visibility difficult at times; forcing Suzie to pull up to set the windscreen in the wide-open position. This, and the canvas awning, helped to lower the temperature when on the move, making driving conditions tolerable.

A very disturbed and angry chief superintendent sat morosely in the passenger seat. He sulked because he had not been able to assert his authority over who should drive first. For an excellent reason Suzie had insisted that she should. He was silent, even when she stopped to let down the awning, where the road entered a rubber estate whose close-planted lineal trees came up to the edge on both sides of the road, forming an arch over the top.

Some ten miles out of Saigon and still in rubber country, but more undulating, the road wound round small hillocks. While negotiating a tight, short bend Suzie changed down and braked to a crawl, snaking her way through the gap between a protruding high bank and fallen rubber tree.

As she skirted the obstacle and turned the jeep hard to the right, a single shot clattered through the trees; Deshampneuf slumped over, almost falling out of the jeep. Blood was everywhere. Suzie struggled in shock to control the vehicle and prevent the body from falling out. Although she knew it was to happen, she was devastated by the gaping hole in the head from which blood flowed: she found herself shaking uncontrollably. Never before had killing been so close, nor had it affected her in this way. She had, after all, enjoyed the companionship of this man, in earlier desperate days.

Benoit emerged from the trees and moved the body to the floor of the jeep. He looked anxiously at Suzie. "You all right?" he asked, noting that her face was drained of all colour and the eyes sunk deep in their sockets.

She nodded limply, "Oui, ça va."

"You know the form," he began. "There's a French company HQ about two kilometres down the road in a fold in the ground on the right-hand side. You'll see camouflage netting over the top. Report the incident and they'll take over the corpse. I've told the lieutenant in charge to expect you. There will be no enquiry—just one of those things."

She looked at his marksman's rifle, "Makes a terrible mess, doesn't it?"

"Russian guerrilla special." He patted it, almost lovingly. "Designed for the job. And, of course, it leaves Russian bullets to be found in the corpse."

"Where will you be?" she asked, almost pleading.

"Right behind you, all the way. Remember—I have to watch over you."

"Thanks." She managed a wan smile.

"Avec plaisir," was his parting compliment, which she loved and drew comfort from as she drove away with her gruesome passenger. Before following her, Benoit removed the tree he had earlier towed with his jeep across the road.

Meanwhile, ahead of them, I was halted by the waters of the magnificent Tonle Sap, the great lake stretching some 150 kilometres from Compong Chuong to Siem Riap. I sat, fascinated by the antics of a lone pelican that had flown in from the west. Repeatedly it dived into the lake, hitting the water with such force the sound reverberated eerily with a muffled rumbling over the lake.

I was amused by its labouring, unsuccessful efforts to return aloft, its catch protruding from both sides of its sack-like bill. "Just like us humans," I thought, "always greedy, trying to take more than we need."

The radio was crackling as I listened for Benoit's call sign, expected at any time about now. Finally the pelican made it aloft just as I heard, "Roadhog to Scotsman—Roadhog to Scotsman—over."

Pressing the handset switch, I acknowledged the call: "Scotsman to Roadhog, receiving."

Benoit was cryptic but clear and signed off with "The lady is well and on her way."

Knowing Deshampneuf was now out of the picture and Suzie was all right, I felt better. There are, however, other things to worry about, notably the Chinese Tongs mentioned by Blitz. They would stop at nothing to prevent this meeting. I am well aware of the cunning of the fanatical Chinese. The extreme French Youth Movement, too, needs watching. There will be others I haven't heard of yet. Stafford May, with radio communications to Saigon, will have news of these, and separate matters, as soon as I reach Siem Riap.

I took comfort in the thought that Suzie was not far behind and I'd see her soon.

The catalogue of the unknown was long and alarming in this almost unique situation and I was aware of the need to be prepared to meet new problems at any time. One of the most unexpected descended upon us as we neared the end of our journey. Torrential rain hampered progress over the last two miles into Siem Riap, developing into an electric storm of terrible violence. Deafening thunderclaps immediately preceded by fork and sheet lightning indicated we were in the centre of two storms, or very near it, at the heart of danger. To make things even more uncomfortable, driving rain entered our vehicles, soaking everything, and visibility down to zero at times forced us to halt periodically.

When finally we reached the Grand Hotel, near to exhaustion, we debussed during a lull, to be welcomed by Hunter, Maryse and Blitz. A great fuss was made of Sieling in his Gurkha uniform—an acknowledgement of the wonderful and brave part he'd played in the operation, acting the part of Professor Lien.

I was concerned for Suzie out there in this storm. It

was my expression that prompted Maryse to ask, "Anything wrong, chéri?"

Side-stepping her question I asked, "What have you found out? Any villains in town?"

"None that we know of, but this morning a light plane landed on the strip, then took off almost immediately. We're checking it out."

"Has Professor Lien contacted his people?"

"I think so. Eddie took him where he wanted to go as soon as we got to the house."

"Good. Paul has the accommodation plan, I suppose?"

"Yes," she confirmed. "He's getting things organised now. Look at him, he's a genius at this sort of thing."

"I'll come to your room later, chérie," I promised. "You have a room here, I hope, as well as the house?"

"Yes, of course," she told me, with emphasis and an expression that left me in no doubt that she, too, knew how to arrange things.

Hunter arrived with the excitable hotel manager, Monsieur Chandel, who wanted to assure me that everything would be done to make Lord Louis's stay perfect, with the understanding that there was to be the minimum of fuss.

Gurkhas' and Signals' commanding officers were found and the business of troop accommodation was agreed, leaving the final allocation of rooms for Lord Louis and his party to be decided later.

I was well pleased with the suite of six rooms Hunter earmarked. I put myself in the middle one. It was important to my plan that Lord Louis had a room to himself, with

Lady Louis apart on the other side of me. Their daughter and the ADC would have two, and Hunter the one at the end of the landing leading to the private entrance.

"If only this bloody rain would ease up," I thought irritably, and decided to discuss plans for tomorrow with Hunter and the Gurkha officer. Signals links with Saigon and Singapore were now established. The Signals' officer reported asking if I had any traffic.

"Yes, I want Captain May, later."

Meanwhile, I decided to check on Maryse's mystery plane that landed that morning, and as the rain eased I left the hotel, making for the airstrip. My enquiries of villagers along the road gave me a good idea who was in the plane; their natural powers of observation and description were superb.

On my return to the hotel, Stafford May came through on the radio with his report, including news of Ulowski and Colonel Shaw leaving Saigon in a light plane. In general, little had changed regarding Franco-British relations and political activities, but May had something very serious to report about Sergeant Fagge. He also reported that an American OSS agent appeared to be talking seriously with Ho Chi-minh. It's rumoured Ho Chi-minh asked for 1,000,000 American soldiers, a very strange request: whom would they fight? James Byrnes, US Secretary of State, declined despite being told the Vietnamese would fight to the death for their independence. Americans were playing the game of "good friend" at the same time with their allies, planning to restore the French to power. These thoughts dominated my mind!

May was alarmed, I could tell by the strangeness of his voice which had taken on a horrified tone, as he worryingly reported. "Gracey has declared martial law, banned public meetings, imposed a curfew and closed down Vietnamese newspapers, while still allowing French press and radio to function. This has upset Vietminh leaders who've mobilised massive protests and demonstrations. The general has insufficient troops to regain control. This has become very serious. To counter possible violent reactions by the Vietminh, Gracey has released all French troops interned by the Japs. These troops have gone on the rampage, looting homes and shops, clubbing men, women and even children indiscriminately. It's chaos. Now we have a general strike called by the Vietminh leaders: Saigon is paralysed—no electricity or water. Shops are shut, offices closed. Even the rickshaws have disappeared from deserted streets."

"OK, Stafford, I've got the picture very clear. Keep me informed as often as you want. It sounds very serious. I should think this will accelerate French control and the departure of Gracey. How secure is our transmission?"

"We're all right, Andrew, I'm on scrambler."

"Thank God." I signed off with, "Take care. By the way, it's best that you call me; if I call you someone else might answer, you understand? Report developments hourly until further notice."

I detailed a Signals' officer to man the radio and to take and record traffic. "I've got the message," he replied with force.

I concealed my fury as I tapped lightly on Maryse's door and heard, "Come in, Andrew."

With my mind totally occupied speculating as to what damage Sergeant Fagge may have done, and this frightful development in Saigon, I needed Maryse now—more as diversion and safety valve.

We talked awhile, one thing leading to another, with no mention of Fagge.

I excused myself. "I've something important to finish off. By the way, it's a hundred-to-one that light plane contained Ulowski and, believe it or not, Colonel 'One-Shot' Shaw."

I closed the door quietly and returned to my room to prepare orders for tomorrow, before turning in.

It was 0230 hours when a tapping on my door awakened me and a voice was saying, "They've arrived, mon colonel." Throwing on my robe I dashed downstairs and there beheld Suzie and Benoit, soaked to the skin despite the storm's abating. It had, as I suspected, moved east, striking them with full force, halting movement and threatening at times to wash them from the road.

I am relieved to see her safe and unhurt, and show it. When I stood back from hugging her, I, too, was soaking wet, my robe acting as a sponge. This amused Benoit whose smile became an infectious laugh bringing relief from suppressed anxiety, to all of us.

Appalling conditions caused Benoit to decide Suzie could not cope alone and, though her pride was hurt, it had been obvious to her that accepting his advice to abandon her jeep and ride with him had probably saved her from serious injury, maybe worse.

"Come up to my room and have a hot bath and a stiff drink," I invited.

At first light I left Suzie snoozing in bed and, with the

Gurkha lieutenant, made for the airstrip to arrange security and guard of honour for Lord Louis.

The sun's rising was seen from a hillock overlooking the runway, and the fresh wet earth and vegetation, washed by the storm, smelt good. The air, cooled by a gentle breeze, disturbed the leaves, sending cold rainwater showering down on bare arms as we moved through the bush. A golden glow flooding the tree-lined horizon made an emotional sight; I had been moved by it hundreds of times before in many mystic lands. *"The day's rebirth has its own inspiration for those of keen perception,"* were words I had heard long ago, always to be recalled when, as now, I was touched by nature's glorious manifestation.

The Gurkha lieutenant's face was alive with the wonder of dawn. Brilliance splashed everywhere, over and through the trees, dressing nature with shape and colour. In his native Nepal such visions have greater spectacle but nature's beauty is the same, varied only by the degree of feeling each has for the moment of revelation.

Both of us took from this wondrous phenomenon the strength of exhilaration that springs from the fresh chance each new day offers. We made our plans, deciding that the hill itself provided the best defensive position. We returned to the hotel and found Monsieur Chandel in his office. Arrangements for cocktail and dinner parties were settled. Monsieur Chandel was, he said, already aware that the Cambodian Royal Dancers would be performing. "We have ways of knowing certain things, colonel," he said with a smile, in answer to my questioning eyes.

Two tasks remained: to see Professor Lien, and to visit Angkor Wat with the Gurkha lieutenant to work out security for the entertainment to be held in the open air.

21

LORD LOUIS'S ARRIVAL in Saigon for the Japanese surrender parade brought to the street crowds of people hungry for glamour and the chance to welcome England's most romantic hero. Particularly for French women, this was something not to be missed. Splendid in white tropical uniform, emblazoned with rows of many-coloured medal ribbons, his handsome head capped in white and gold, brought cheers ringing continuously from the airport to the Palais de L'Indo-Chine. Here was a man who had it all: good looks, rank, a princely background; without doubt, the most romantically glamorous Supreme Allied Commander among the Western Allies.

This great surrender parade, with rank upon rank of Japanese troops advancing to the flag-draped tables, preceded by their officers, went on for two hours. Each Japanese officer handing over his Samurai sword to his British opposite number was performed with military precision of the highest order. The British officer in charge of organising things had cleverly charged the Japanese with this responsibility, the result was total success. It seemed once the Japanese had accepted defeat, surrendering was to be militarily perfect.

Major Tomita had earlier surrendered his sword to me, before his imprisonment.

The Japanese Supreme Commander however was, due to ill health, absent from this parade. Later, behind Gracey's HQ that evening, an elderly and defeated Field Marshal Count Terauchi sat in a wheelchair, accompanied by his chief of staff and ADC, to await the arrival of Britain's Supreme Allied Commander, South East Asia, Admiral Mountbatten.

All was quiet except for the rustle of leaves and the humming birds darting from one nectar to the next. Lord Louis stepped through the french windows onto the patio and slowly, with his aides, descended the steps to the lawn. Major-General Gracey attended as head of mission and Captain Gunn, RN, as military adviser. Senior staff officers of the three services sprang to attention, saluting as Lord Louis took up his position.

Brigadier Mandell made a short announcement, which was repeated in Japanese, whereupon Field Marshal Count Terauchi was wheeled forward. War correspondents' cameras clicked as he reached the table covered with a Union Jack. An aide handed Terauchi two swords, one at a time, which he in turn surrendered to Lord Louis; the first, his long, curved Samurai sword, the second, a ceremonial piece—much shorter. Both were sheathed, signifying they should not be returned. In fifteen minutes all was over and the old warrior tyrant was wheeled sadly away.

Lord Louis said goodbye to Major-General Gracey and left for the airport and the short flight to Siem Riap.

It was 1900 hours as the RAF Dakota banked for turning into the approach; a few minutes later its wheels brushed the tarmac, bouncing lightly into its run-up to the wooden shack serving as terminal building and control tower. Siem Riap airfield is protected by Gurkha soldiers, inconspicuously stationed around the perimeter, and on the high ground.

A Gurkha guard of honour stands to attention, presenting arms at the precise moment Lord Louis alights from the plane. Lady Louis followed, ahead of her daughter and ADC. I welcome the visitors and introduce to Lord Louis the Gurkha lieutenant, who invited the admiral to review the guard.

The inspection over, our guests are carried away by the French district commissioner in his very old but handsome and immaculate De Dion limousine, which both surprised and delighted the Mountbattens.

Monsieur Chandel, the hotel manager, and his wife, receive us in old baronial style; the staff lined up as welcoming party. Lady Louis is scintillated, using the moment to practise her French with a few words to each.

Lord Louis caught my eye. "What have you laid on for us other than this dancing show tonight?"

"A small cocktail party, followed by an even smaller dinner for the local dignitaries."

"That's all, I hope," said Lord Louis apprehensively. "We came here to get away from the social round! You know that. The most important happening is this meeting with Ho Chi-minh."

"That's all," I assured him.

"Edwina," raising his voice slightly Mountbatten called to his wife; and to me said, "She gets so enthusiastic on these occasions, I have to calm her. It's good for public relations but hard on the patience."

Lady Louis was free at last and they went to their rooms. "See you in half an hour, colonel," said Lord Louis from halfway up the staircase.

❧

Relaxed and refreshed, Lord Louis was mixing drinks, I could tell by the tinkle of ice. I tapped on his door, but he went on with the preparation as he called, "Come in."

He looked at me coming across the room—wondering if something was amiss. "Something wrong?" he asked.

"No, sir," I replied, to correct the impression my face gave. "I'm preoccupied with the deception plan, the risk I'm exposing Sie-ling to." I was, of course, concerned about the presence of Ulowski and Colonel Shaw, but had no intention of telling Lord Louis—it could only serve to alarm a situation I had fully under control.

"Tell me about it," said Lord Louis.

I outlined my plan, which was to draw attention away from Lord Louis's room, and the part Sie-ling would play, in offering himself as Ho Chi-minh in decoy.

"I see," said Lord Louis. "There is considerable danger for him. It has to be, I suppose?"

"Oh yes," I confirmed. "Without this, there's no way of diverting attention from those opposed to the meeting."

"You spoke of a possibility that Ho may simply be kidnapped with no harm coming to him. How likely is that?" asked Lord Louis with much concern in his voice.

"It's likely, all depends on who gets their hands on him.

The French would abduct him, whereas the Russians and Chinese have other ways of using a valuable hostage."

"So we go ahead as planned?"

"Yes, sir!" I said with absolute certainty.

Comfortable in his bush jacket, the admiral poured me a drink and slipped into a commodious bamboo chair. We talked about forthcoming events with a calmness that belied inner doubts. Timing was important if a leak had occurred. It was particularly critical if, expecting an attack at the private entrance, it came at Lord Louis's room.

"But we've no evidence there will be an attack," said Lord Louis. "There's no reason to believe anyone knows of the meeting. I realise that care and precaution are necessary. Have you something stronger than suspicion?"

"In this setting, word will get out somehow, or intelligent guessing will have worked it out that your visit here is not as innocent as it looks. Particularly if Ho has been watched and seen to come here."

Mountbatten nodded his head, "OK, colonel, it's your show. Just tell me what I'm to do."

Stafford May's words, "Something very serious to report about Sergeant Fagge," were alarming but the one thing I had to avoid was panic. Until I knew more about it nothing would be said to Lord Louis. As to the troubles in Saigon, Lord Louis would know of them already, having been there himself, today.

The chief Signals' officer found me at the hotel bar with Monsieur Chandel. His appearance was glum.

He said with anxiety in his voice, "Captain May's on the line, sir."

I hurried to the radio room we'd set up at the back of the hotel.

"Hello, Stafford, what's new?"

"I think the general's lost his nerve. He's issuing edicts right, left and centre. It's hard to know who's in command," Stafford said calmly. "There's a group called Binh Xuyen, a kind of Mafia who hire themselves out like mercenaries; and a Frenchman Jean Cédile, sent out by de Gaulle as his representative. Cédile has refused to accept Vietminh's demands for sovereignty. He's apparently under the influence of French merchants—planters and officials who insist that Cédile takes a hard line with the Viets, who they derisively call agitators and bandits. Cédile has now antagonised the Vietminh by denouncing them and ordering them to obey the French. Most serious is—Gracey's finally shown his colours. He's exceeded his instructions by proclaiming his desire for the French to return. Admiral Mountbatten, you remember, told the general to keep clear of politics and Indo-China's internal affairs. I think he's shot his bolt!"

"This is bound to offend China and Russia, Whitehall will be furious with him," I replied. "The general's made a bad diplomatic mistake. Keep me posted of developments. Call me at any time if things worsen."

I'm now wondering if it's wise to proceed with this meeting of Mountbatten and Ho Chi-minh. The political situation appears to have changed dramatically in Saigon.

But, the cause we serve is of such tremendous importance to the principle that when great, powerful nations are fearful of a small nation's political policies, like communism, they do not have a moral or other right to use their military might to bring about change.

We can't stop now; the alternative is too dreadful to contemplate—war involving America, France, China and Russia to save Vietnam.

22

ANGKOR WAT IS like fairyland. The long promenade leading to the magnificently fluted spires of the temple is aglow with dancing flames of torches held by 200 youths lining each balustrade. The strange music played by priests on string and wind instruments, in half and quarter tones, is to the Western ear new and full of mystery. This was the haunting introduction to the Cambodian Royal Dancers' *pièce de résistance*, setting a scene and atmosphere of enchantment.

As the honoured guests arrived and settled in the front row of the audience, with me seated beside Lord Louis, the music grew louder and the young torch-bearers performed delicate and artistic acts of passing torches in such a way, when spinning they resembled Catherine wheels.

Then came the dancers whose unique routine was that reserved for royalty. It was a simple story of romance between prince and princess. The museum's curator explained to Lady Louis the meaning of each lasciviously seductive movement, and she was obviously enjoying this ancient and colourful spectacle, which held everyone spellbound for nearly two delightful hours of magical moments.

Performers wore costume jewellery and colourful theatrical ornaments, each glinting in the torchlight as they moved. Music changed key and tempo at intervals, building to a climax, when the leading dancer surprisingly lay prostrate in the centre of a semi-circle formed by other dancers. Torches waved in unison, describing diverse patterns until, suddenly, all was silent; nothing moved except the flames reaching higher as if to lick the sky.

Gradually the leader began her slow finale. It was like a slow-motion exercise at first; dance and music in unison and sympathy, then, to sharp staccato movements, she progressed slowly towards Lord Louis, grovelling on her belly the last few feet. Once again the curator described it to us: "When she reaches you," he said to Lord Louis, "take what she has in her hands. It is her total submission— the princess to the prince. Symbolically, of course, sir," he added seriously.

"Of course," said Lord Louis, having a quiet chuckle to himself.

Now almost at Lord Louis's feet, the dancer loosened her long tresses, removing the hair ornaments. Coming to rest in front of him on her knees, her head thrown forward with arms outstretched, she offered the trinkets.

As the only light is from the torch flames, nothing can be seen clearly; even the audience is an indistinct group, and the dancers just vague statues in exquisite poses.

We could just make out the hands and metal objects, which Mountbatten received one by one, gingerly, and laid in his lap. The last piece was the main ivory comb which held the dancer's hair high. In the flickering of the torchlight, and looking sideways to the comb, I could see something odd jammed between its teeth. I removed it with conjurer's dexterity—an involuntary reflex when faced by surprise—and concealed it in my loosely closed hand. Instinctively I felt it to be sinister, whatever it was.

"Now give them back to her, sir, one at a time," requested the curator, "and she will finish her act."

Mountbatten returned the articles one by one and the scene went wild; music became louder and quicker as the dancers gyrated in what was afterwards described as the dance of seduction.

Everyone was thrilled by the beauty of this simple love story, which performed in dark of night was haunting magic, a mystique pervading the scene.

Flaming torches, so artistically spun and waved to the rhythm of oriental music was enchanting.

"C'est merveilleuse!" exclaimed Lady Louis.

"Oui, oui," replied a chorus of happy voices.

"C'est belle," added the wife of the curator.

23

I LEFT SUZIE asleep and went to my bedroom to keep an urgent appointment with Paul Hunter.

"Come in," I replied to the familiar tap on the door. "Had breakfast?"

"Not yet." Hunter closed the door.

"Good. I've ordered for two."

"What's so important?" Hunter asked, sinking into a well upholstered rattan chair. I sat on the bed facing him, knowing that I was about to shatter my friend.

"You know Madame Bastien, I believe. Rather intimately, I understand?"

Hunter naturally wondered what this was all about. He replied as normally as possible, "Yes, why do you ask?"

"Because Madame Bastien is both spying for Russia and being your mistress at the same time—according to Suzie Barbancourt."

Hunter's look of disbelief fell full upon me; shaken, he challenged with, "You're not serious?" knowing full well that I never joked about important things.

"Suzie stumbled onto it when checking on the leak at the Joint Council. Madame Bastien was seen visiting the spy Raoul Fournier, the council's secretary. Suzie followed her to several places and on each occasion Ulowski was present."

Hunter was about to speak but I was not finished. "We have another bad egg in our basket, which is even more worrying. Stafford reports that Sergeant Fagge has been caught red-handed passing information to Madame Bastien and he has made a full confession."

"For Christ's sake," burst Hunter, "what's happening to us?"

"Unbelievable, I know. We took Fagge for granted, didn't we? No screening because he'd been with the general for so long. Had we checked we'd have found that Fagge has a penchant for little boys' arseholes, particularly the virgin ones." I was angry with myself for this blunder.

"You'd never have guessed," gasped Hunter. "It never showed. What does all this mean, Andrew? How much damage has been done?"

"Stafford's built a case for me to study and I hope to have this in a signal tonight. Meanwhile, I know that Ulowski and Colonel Shaw were in the light plane Maryse reported on when we arrived. No doubt they got information from Fagge."

"This will break up the general, he's become very much attached to Fagge and trusted him completely—almost as a son."

I decided to tell Hunter more, this new development required it. I explained about Colonel Shaw and the part he played in Drury's death: how Shaw had been disgraced over collaboration with the Japs and finally gone in with the Russians.

Now was also the moment to confide to Hunter the other

half of the deception plan. Hunter knew about Sie-ling's role, but he believed that Ho Chi-minh and Professor Lien would themselves enter the front door disguised as Catholic priests.

"This cannot go ahead now, Paul," I explained. "It's too risky. As soon as I had word of Fagge's perfidy I contacted Lien and the plan was changed. Two 'priests' will still come as arranged but they will be plants, not Ho and Lien. Ho and Lien will remain at their hideout until I give them the all-clear."

"Apart from this," Hunter asked, "the plan goes ahead?"

"Yes. I can see no point in changing things, can you? We're not beaten yet!"

"No. It's our last throw of the dice, let's go for it."

"From now on, have Benoit and Dawney on my tail day and night. *I'm* now the target they need, to prevent the meeting taking place."

I gave Hunter the note I'd plucked from the dancer's comb. It told of a plan to kidnap me. "If they can snatch me from the scene they think this will shut things down. Here's where they're wrong, because you'll be there to carry on. Put your best men with Sie-ling and give one of them the Russian revolver we took from the guerrillas. If anyone's shot let Russian bullets be found in the body at a medical enquiry."

My tone of voice left Hunter with no alternative but to obey. He knew there was no way he could influence the course that events would now follow, apart from voicing his fears for my safety.

I continued: "This is now something we play by ear, Paul. To do otherwise would be madness on our part. Fagge knew almost everything, and we must assume that he informed Ulowski. What I don't understand is how Ulowski got away from detention in the Sureté. It looks like the French have a few reds in their police who have disobeyed Deshampneuf's order to hold Ulowski until our return."

"In all probability," suggested Hunter, "they know of Deshampneuf's death and their new man has different ideas."

"Maybe," I replied, "but we're working blind from now on, and this calls for that something special we have in reserve. Increase the Gurkha guard around the hotel immediately!"

Finally, I revealed Stafford May's report on Gracey's loss of control in Saigon; of the general strike of civil servants, cutting off electricity and water, producing civil disobedience. Worst of all was the premature release of French troops from internment by the Japs; they had gone on a rampage, looting and raping, resulting in a breakdown of law and order.

Gracey had proclaimed his support for French control in Indo-China.

"We'll discuss this more, later," I said, "and I'm not telling Lord Louis at this stage. Come, let's be off parade for a few hours, relax and enjoy a social evening with some locals at the party tonight. Maryse is coming, she has a home here, and may pick up something useful about the political future of the country."

The cocktail party was a success from all points of view. There were some forty local notaries, most of whom were interned by the Japanese and subjected to cruel indignities. They relished this wonderful moment of close association with one so famous—virtually the liberator of themselves and their country.

With Gurkhas on security guard, their kukris ever ready should the careless and foolhardy try something, it was not surprising that there were no incidents. Although, according to Monsieur Chandel, one or two of those attending had shown adverse tendencies towards the Japanese, no evidence of anti-British feeling was seen. In fact, reported Maryse—so clever at drawing people out—such criticisms as were made were against the French civil servants who, it seemed, had ingratiated themselves with the enemy at the expense of the populace. Many had been arrested and abused on the word of a government officer who, in return, enjoyed freedom and privileges.

Lady Louis, as always, charmed them with amusing anecdotes of her work, by solicitous enquiries of local affairs and problems in particular.

I watched her move from one group to another and wondered what the real Edwina was like. My background information on her was sketchy in certain areas with spicy speculative stories of waywardness. That she had sympathies with socialism ample evidence prevailed. How, I wondered, had one so rich and fond of her rank and social position reconciled her politics with her privileged place in the world? It was that chance remark in Singapore that alerted me to ask Peter Bain for further information on the lady. It was good information, supporting my belief that she would be sympathetic to the indigenous people's desire for independence. Odd, I thought, that I had run a security check on Edwina but not on Fagge!

The dinner party was a simple compliment to a few French and Vietnamese officials responsible for local government, including the director of the museum and the Ruins of Angkor Wat—the ancient temple of the Kmer civilisation of the third century. It was simply the usual diplomatic courtesy function, not designed to produce anything other than good international relations. It was also an opportunity for the Mountbattens to sound out local opinion about the future of the country, through the eyes of a cross-section of those to whom it was of greatest importance.

It was 2115 when Lord Louis caught my eye and indicated it was time to go. I relayed the message to Lady Louis, my table companion, who asked if the ladies should leave the gentlemen—as in England.

"No. Lord Louis wants to go now. He has signals from London and Singapore to deal with." I said this to hide the fact that Lord Louis and I had much to discuss of the night's secret activities.

"OK," she accepted and got up, indicating that dinner was over. Words were not necessary as everyone followed her lead. In the grand hall the Mountbattens spent some time saying their goodbyes, then went to their rooms.

My night was just beginning, but first I had to explain a few things to the Mountbatten girl and ADC. I had to ensure that they remained in their rooms no matter what might happen later this night. Up to now they had been told nothing of the proposed meeting, in accordance with my policy of never telling *all* until operationally right to do so.

I outlined the general plan and its important purpose— to bring Ho Chi-Minh together with Lord Louis in an attempt to avert civil war. They gave it their blessing.

"If you hear loud noises or even shooting, you must remain inside your rooms. There's nothing you can do to help and you might upset things by appearing… especially if you're taken hostage!"

They got the message and assured me that they would stay put, though they would worry like hell. I quietly saluted this night with the remains of my drink and left them sitting at the bar. "Bloody hell! They kept this one secret, didn't they?" I heard the ADC say.

At Maryse's house I gathered my team around me and asked for up-to-the-minute reports from each. I needed every scrap of information for the final report to Lord Louis before the show began.

Hunter's men had been active in the disputed territories on the border between Siam and Cambodia, and around Battambang, Sisaphon to the north-west and Pailin to the south-west, and all along the border. They had made contact with British Intelligence units at Battambang, who reported intense communist activity. Village headmen had been coerced into believing that life could be more rewarding for them under a socialist system, while many simple folk had come to accept the rewards of loyal service to Mao Tse-tung's concept of the ideal state. Without doubt the whole area had been exploited most successfully by the communists.

Blitz had plenty of proof that local-government officers, schoolteachers and those in the professions, including some French expatriates, were inclining to what was being called "progressive thinking". Clearly, nationalism was receiving wide support for the political and social change that was inevitable under communism.

Maryse described two men, villagers had seen land by light plane that morning. I told her I already knew they were Ulowski and the American Colonel Shaw.

"So," I said, "we can expect trouble from them as well as others. But the plan goes ahead—there's no point in making changes now."

24

I AM NOW convinced that within the hour an attempt will be made to snatch me. I knew, apart from a preliminary roughing-up, I would be fairly safe—all they wanted from me was to know about the meeting. They needed to stop it. With luck they would keep me alive for some time, giving Hunter and the others time to turn tables; my stalling tactics would lengthen the breathing space.

I decided there would be plenty of time before the event to test the opposition. I went looking for Hunter and Dawney, my shadows, who had followed me from the hotel. We made rough plans for action in certain circumstances.

"Don't act immediately when I'm accosted: let them believe no one knows they've got me; keep out of sight and follow to where I'm taken; do a reconnaissance and make your plan accordingly," I instructed. "I'm going along with this so as to know who we're up against and, with your help, to eliminate them."

"OK," said Hunter.

He watched me move out of the shadows from the rear of the house and drive my jeep towards the roadway.

Turning onto the road from the rough ground I moved slowly through the gears. In the dark I saw three men in slouch hats, and took comfort from having some of Hunter's men keeping watch on the house. At that moment one raised a hand, as I mistakenly thought, to check my identity.

"Move over, colonel," ordered the big man standing to the right of the one pointing his automatic at my gut. "I'll drive and we'll have a little chat somewhere cosy and quiet."

I knew the voice from long ago. It belonged to one I had collaborated with against the Japanese.

Bugger!

It had been in Laos in my early guerrilla days, soon after the Japs took over the country.

"Well, well," I said mockingly. "So, you've returned to the scene."

Colonel Yuri Grekowski is one of the Soviet's toughest operatives. He already knew of my skills so would take special precautions.

"Yes, my friend. I must congratulate you on your promotion. But you've a long way to go to match our offer. I told you long ago that if you worked for us you would be full colonel, and later, who knows, maybe a general." He gave a signal and the third man frisked me, taking my Belgian automatic.

Grekowski, driving at moderate speed, and in what seemed to be good humour, told me, as he had so many times, "The British always failed to appreciate your qualities, so why work for the lowest bidder?"

"That's something you'll never understand, Yuri," I replied, "and I'll not try to educate you. But when the time comes, as it will, and you seek asylum in the West, let me know, and I'll see what can be done."

Yuri Grekowski appeared outwardly amused, but inside he raged at the insult. He roared with mock laughter, and looking at me, spat out, "You cheeky bastard!" He drove on for about two miles to a signpost pointing to the right but with no name on it. Without a noticeable slackening of speed he turned to the right, following a track leading into a rubber estate. After five minutes he braked at the rear of a single-storey bungalow out of sight of the track.

One man remained on guard while the other two escorted me inside the bungalow.

"Go and watch the front," ordered Grekowski, and he was alone with his prisoner. At that moment, the whole area around the bungalow was flooded in light rendering it impossible either to approach or leave the building without being seen.

In a spacious and tastefully furnished room, Grekowski became very, almost ridiculously, friendly. He invited me to be comfortable and have a drink. I knew that this happy situation would not last and judged it wise to play along with the charade and see what happened.

"What's all this about, Yuri?" I asked. "You've made a balls-up, haven't you?"

"No, my friend," replied Grekowski in calm and mellow tones. "We're going to discuss this meeting you've arranged between Admiral Mountbatten and Ho Chi-minh. We know it has to happen tonight because the admiral leaves tomorrow and it didn't take place last night."

I studied this powerful man of good looks and ideal proportions, now the wrong side of forty but still the perfect physical specimen. His smiling face held a confidence that might intimidate a lesser man. Now, as I inwardly cursed Fagge for this situation, I surreptitiously studied the room for any means of escape.

I wondered where my watchers were and what plan they had for turning the tables on Yuri. I couldn't imagine how they could cross, unseen, the floodlit open space around the bungalow.

"You've gone mad," I decided to try. "Who's been telling you silly stories? Why would such a meeting be arranged? And tell me, if you can, how would we benefit from such an event?"

The Russian wore the same smile, knowing he hadn't much time to work on me. He stroked his cleft chin and casually pushed back a wayward lock of black hair, his thoughts obviously fixed on ways of making me tell all.

"You've heard of Boris Ulowski, I believe," he said calmly, with emphasis. "Boris discovered enough before being picked up by the French. A very astute man is Boris. For example, your two meetings with Professor Lien and the one you didn't keep when Captain Hunter acted for you. Then your reply to the message delivered by a Corporal Evans to Lien. Boris decided that all this was very important."

"So," I said, "what's all this got to do with a meeting between Mountbatten and Ho?"

"Be patient, my friend," admonished Grekowski, "I shall tell you all. Boris cleverly decided, after your first meeting, to step up surveillance on both you and Lien. As expected you became cautious but Lien had no such inhibitions. Believing his plans secure and well laid, he attended a meeting at the Sun Wah Restaurant in Cholon." Grekowski paused, looking at me for reaction, for some telltale signs.

Finding none, he went on, "Do you know who else was at that meeting, my friend?"

"No," I said, apprehensive at the way things were going.

"As I thought," snapped the Russian. "You really don't know, I can hear it in your voice—that unmistakable honesty, so rare in our business! Then let me inform you of the VIPs Boris saw with Lien in that top-floor room. It was a remarkable array: Ho Chi-minh, Mao Tse-tung and Lin Shao-chi! Now, if *you* were sitting on the roof next door, looking through the window at this gathering, what conclusion would you come to?"

This suited me well and I hoped Grekowski would use up enough time in this way to allow for Hunter to get things organised.

"How would *I* know?" I replied, letting astonishment into my voice. "A meeting of these important men is way over *my* head. Why shouldn't they meet and discuss the future of this country, after all, they are contiguous with common borders so what happens here must be important to the Chinese. And, in any case, they're all communists."

"But," Grekowski countered, "Boris saw another, not as high and mighty as the others, but just as important, if you know who he represents."

"Who?"

"Major Lim Teng-moi, right-hand man to Chiang Kai-shek. Now what do we make of that, my friend? Ideological enemies sitting down together!"

"I don't have a clue about it," I insisted.

"Well," Grekowski said slowly, "we could conclude that, after two meetings with you, and who knows, a few hand-delivered messages, Professor Lien is reporting to these gentlemen on progress he has made in a deal you've had a hand in."

"Rubbish!" I exploded, in a louder voice. "What possible interest have I in Lien's chats with these people?"

My keen ear heard a change in the volume of sound made by the electric generator; for an instant the phut-phut of the diesel engine grew louder, then back to normal, as if the powerhouse door had opened and shut.

"This is no longer a mystery, my friend," Grekowski said sternly, "We believe you're part of a conspiracy with Ho and the Chinese, and this meeting was an exchange of undertakings and guarantees. I believe that you're doing a deal which excludes the Soviet Union—we cannot allow this."

The last words were almost drowned by the crack of rifle fire as the lights went out. For a split second all was black; quickly my eyes adjusted; with the help of bright moonlight it was possible to pick out my escape route.

I scrambled through an open window onto the verandah surrounding the building. Grekowski was shouting and swearing in Russian, with the guard answering. I made for the back door and found the guard by the flash of his gunfire. Moving swiftly, I sank the stiletto—I'd concealed it in my bush hat—up to the hilt under the left shoulder blade, angled so as to pierce the heart.

I caught the gun of the big Russian as he crashed down, and leapt over him to face the doorway as Grekowski came through. I squeezed the trigger, hitting the target clean through the forehead, boring a large hole as the lead bullet spread on impact before passing through the brain and out the back of the head.

Suddenly, the verandah was flooded in light from a jeep's headlamps, and the deafening explosion of a rifle not far from my right ear was followed by an indistinct but familiar sound as my eyes registered the collapse of a mass of man into a heap on the verandah planking in front of me.

"You all right?" came the sound, now recognisable as Suzie's anxious voice. "I had to shoot him or he'd have killed you. Sorry about your ear—hope the drum's not shattered."

"How the hell did you get into this?" I asked, relieved to see Sergeant-Major Dawney swinging himself over the verandah railing and pulling Suzie up too. Impulsively, I put my arms round her and said, "Thanks for saving my life. You shall have your reward." I hoped to convey more than mere words.

She grinned back at me. The physical contact both soothed and excited us—we wanted each other desperately. She replied, "I'm your self-appointed bodyguard. I was chosen because I'm the only one small enough to crawl through a monsoon drainpipe and along a trench, unseen, to the powerhouse to pull the switch."

"OK," I said as Dawney and Benoit returned, reporting the house now safe. "I've a date with Lord Louis. Better see what papers these comrades have, before disposing of the bodies."

❧

"I'm worried about Sie-ling," said Suzie, sitting beside me in the jeep as we returned to the hotel. "He's such a nice man and so sincere about his people, it would be terrible if he were killed."

As always the voice was the giveaway, her concern was obvious in the tone and in the gaps in the wrong places, due to breathlessness and anxiety.

"Don't worry," I comforted, "we're not letting anything happen to Sie-ling, and, besides, he's no fool. He knows how to handle situations like this. Our plan is so tight that there's only one place where he will be at risk."

Benoit, sitting in the back, reassured her, "We've so many sharpshooters covering the area that risk is reduced to the minimum."

Suzie knew fear—and bravery too. Fear had been her constant companion in France, with the Resistance. It was this that excited her about Sie-ling, who showed no trace of fear. So many times he had told her of the shadow hanging over his people if unbridled nationalism took over in Indo-China and the policy of ethnic cleansing prevailed.

She knew of his dedication to preventing this happening by all means open to him. Sie-ling knew the risks involved, but of no alternative course to take. From the beginning, he innately knew that a prearranged deal with Ho was essential to the well-being of thousands of expatriate Chinese long resident in the country. Some form of monitored independence under the watchful eyes of Britain and China was necessary to ensure the orderly resettlement of those wishing to leave the country over a phased period of time.

Sie-ling knew that if de Gaulle insisted on retaining French sovereignty over the country by placing it within the French Union, or even partitioning so as to keep hold of the south, war was inevitable. War, with all its pain and eventual misery for his people.

All this had persuaded Suzie of the justice behind what she was now part of, and sustained her in her breach of responsibility to her country.

25

THE SUPREME ALLIED Commander was reading messages from Singapore and London when I arrived. "Fix yourself a drink," he invited, "I'll only be a couple of minutes."

I poured scotch onto some crushed ice, and decided not to tell the admiral about the kidnapping. "Nothing from London yet?" I asked.

Lord Louis looked up, questioningly.

"About de Gaulle's possible intentions?" I explained, relaxing into a bamboo chair.

"No, not so far," he replied. "Everything ready for tonight?" asked Lord Louis, flipping over the last signal and adding a note on the flysheet.

"All set to go, sir."

The admiral closed the file. "That's finished," he said. He poured himself a stiff measure of scotch onto cracked ice then filled the tall glass with ginger ale, cut a thick slice of wild orange, nicked the rind and draped it over the rim of the glass, letting the tangy juices trickle into the cool liquid.

"Lady Louis is very excited about this meeting," he remarked, sliding into a long chair beside me. "She's read everything available in Singapore about Ho, now she's a blooming expert on him!"

We both smiled, knowing that nobody would ever know much about Ho Chi-minh, probably the most enigmatic man of power.

"You know the form?" I said for final confirmation. "You and Lady Louis go into my room just before 2230 hours. Dawney, assisted by two Gurkhas, will receive two 'priests', in your room. He will report their arrival to you, but you will not make contact until I give the word."

"Meanwhile," broke in Mountbatten, "you will be watching over brave Sie-ling as he attracts the villains to himself at the rear of the building; how great a risk is he running, Andrew?" Using my first name showed the tension we all felt.

"Don't know the answer to that, sir. Depends on the extent of action to stop Ho getting to you. I've based my plan on preventing a shootout, but the risk remains that I may have overlooked something. I hope not."

"You're really counting on it being a snatch, aren't you? You thought they'd keep it quiet so as not to tangle with the Gurkhas and their kukris, I remember you saying."

I nodded, "But, if someone wants Ho dead anyway, this is the golden opportunity." I looked at my watch. "Time to go," I added, as the communicating door opened and Lady Louis came in. Both of us got up. Lady Louis, smiling, approached me.

"This is one of those great moments in history that will never be recorded," she began. "Just think what hangs on it, whichever way it goes. Good luck, Colonel Grant," she extended both hands to me, sensing the moment's need for physical contact to reinforce resolve. "Good luck, too, to that brave Sie-ling."

"We'll be waiting for you," said Lord Louis. "Come to us as soon as you can when your show is over. Take care, Andrew, there's so much more for you to do."

Paul Hunter stood at the bottom of the staircase in the main hall as arranged. To show him I was physically fit after the kidnapping, I moved swiftly to join him.

Crossing the marble floor, we turned to reach the rear exit leading to the ground-floor verandah. I looked back on reaching the doorway, in time to see two nondescript Catholic priests enter the hotel by the main door—as expected.

Once on the flagstones of the verandah, a right-hand turn led onto a pathway fringing the open space where danger lay. This brought us unseen to the assembly point where Sie-ling, Maryse, Blitz and Suzie waited in the shadows, with two others dressed like priests.

"Go!" I told Maryse. "Stay well to the right of the walkway."

When she was 200 paces out, Blitz went ahead, having been briefed to stop her midway and start arguing. Sie-ling (disguised as Ho Chi-minh), with his two priestly companions, had been watching Maryse and Blitz. "Wait for them to meet, then all three of you stroll along the walkway. You know the rest has to depend on events. Good luck."

Maryse neared the place where Blitz would catch her up and accost her. At that moment they scuffle and this is Suzie's cue to run to Maryse's aid. I hoped this diversion would unbalance anyone looking for Ho Chi-minh, and enable Sie-ling to reach the point where he would be safe from any sniper in a fixed position. From then on shooting would be unlikely and a snatch more probable.

I wanted all this to cause movement which my many Gurkha eyes and ears could spot. I surveyed the scene with Hunter. All my players were on stage. Sie-ling and party were progressing along the walkway and the pseudo-argument was in full swing halfway between Sie-ling and the danger zone. No movement and no action by the enemy—and Sie-ling was almost at the private entrance.

"Let's go," I indicated to Hunter, with a thrust of my shoulder. The next danger point is the arbour housing the private entrance, where someone may be hiding for the snatch.

As we ran, the others were converging on the arbour, the "family row" had vanished as the players, their guns at the ready, raced to support Sie-ling. I saw all this and quickened pace to be there in time. With barely fifty paces to go, I caught sight of Hunter unexpectedly racing after two figures running from beyond the arbour. He then changed course, and taking four Gurkhas with him was seen heading for a small wooden building on the edge of the open space. They went at great speed and fanned out, disappearing into the scrub and the trees beyond.

I reached the arbour seconds before Maryse and Blitz, to find Sie-ling surveying the area. "There's no one here!" he said in surprise. "But I'm sure I saw two men in what looked like monks' habits run out of the arbour as I approached."

Rapidly reassessing the situation, I concluded that any

attempt would now come from the front. Quickly I unlocked the private door leading from the arbour to the back staircase; I detailed Maryse and Blitz to reinforce the Gurkhas hidden in the main hall. Sie-ling, his two attendants, Suzie and I went to the back stairs that served the suite of rooms occupied by the Mountbattens.

Charging up, we reached the landing in time to see a maid approaching Lord Louis's room. She carried a tray and was accompanied by two Asian-looking men dressed as servants. Their eyes were nervously all-seeing. I knew this had to be phoney, a clumsy attempt at deception, for no one would have ordered room service at this time of night, of all nights.

"This is it," I whispered to Sie-ling. "As soon as Dawney hears a knock on the door he will grab whoever is there, then we go in with our knives ready." And to Suzie: "You're the backup if things go wrong. Just shoot to kill."

At that moment, the maid disappeared through the doorway—dragged in by Sergeant-Major Dawney, who closed the door hard, shutting out the thugs.

It happened rapidly. As the two men were trying to force open the door, Sie-ling and I sprang from cover, burying our long blades deep into their backs as they collapsed dead—or seriously wounded.

Suzie covered me as I called to Dawney to open up. With Sie-ling I entered the room to find the maid out cold on the floor, from Dawney's well delivered chop to the side of the neck. The tray with its scattered contents revealed a revolver, which Dawney picked up and made safe.

I moved closer for, in some strange way, the figure was not unfamiliar. I turned the maid's head and a wig fell away revealing a young face obviously made up to resemble a

Vietnamese. Suzie, the expert at makeup, came forward and declared it very good.

"Clean her up," I ordered. "Let's see what she looks like with her own face."

Using a towel and some of Lady Louis's face cream Suzie finished just as the maid came to.

"My God!" I exclaimed, looking down at Marie-Claire Simone. Never had I reckoned on her going this far to achieve the aims of the Youth Movement. Such bloody-fool boldness and daring was, I thought, completely out of character. But, obviously, you never know with women, particularly those of mixed race threatened with expulsion from the country of their birth.

"Look who's here," I said to those just arrived from below. Maryse was first through the door and, seeing me kneeling, asked if I was all right.

"I'm OK, but this maid isn't."

"Mon dieu!" Maryse exclaimed, coming closer. "Little Marie-Claire—a wild-eyed guerrilla!"

Marie-Claire had recovered sufficiently to swear in response, but her further abuses were drowned by a commotion in the hall below, caused by the noisy arrival of Hunter and his Gurkhas.

Looking from the balcony, I saw what I'd half-expected from Paul's sudden dash off into the dark. Two prisoners dressed from head to foot in camouflage clothing. Hunter wore his wonderful smile of self-satisfaction.

"See who's here?" he called up to me, removing the monk-like hoods from the prisoners. "Strange companions, n'est-ce pas?"

"Colonel Shaw and Comrade Ulowski." I was not surprised. "Hang on to them, Paul, I'll be down soon."

216

Suzie took charge of Marie-Claire while Sergeant-Major Dawney began the business of having the dead bodies removed.

I went to reassure Lord and Lady Louis. "Sorry about that little rumpus. My stage setting to draw them to the private entrance didn't work. They didn't fall for it, so the showdown had to be outside your door." I broadly outlined the events, explaining about the use of doubles.

"Phoneys and doubles!" Lady Louis exclaimed. "You mean these two aren't really Ho and Lien?" Both Mountbattens registered disbelief and it was Lady Louis who demanded severely: "Whatever does this mean, Colonel Grant; whose deception is this?"

Lord Louis was chuckling. He remembered me telling him in Singapore about Ho's official doubles.

"You see, my dear," he began, "this is typical caution of Colonel Grant. I should have recalled sooner. He told me about this when he came to Singapore. Ho has several official doubles who appear as him in tricky situations, such as this. The colonel probably knew of this, but, as usual, he never tells all in case someone speaks out of turn and fouls things up. Obviously, Ho sent doubles in case of trouble. Rather like the old-time food-tasters."

"You never told me about Ho using doubles," she chided him. "But how clever. If anyone's to die it's the double! I like that. Why don't we have doubles, Dickie? Wouldn't be British, would it! You really are a devious fellow, Andrew Grant."

"So," said Mountbatten, "we just wait for the real Ho to come. Will he come tonight, Andrew?"

"Yes, sir," I replied, opening the communicating door and beckoning to the doubles to follow. "I'll make it as quick as possible."

❧

Before we could get through the door, the senior Signals' officer arrived in haste and agitation carrying a message, his usually jovial countenance very glum.

"That from London?" I asked.

"Yes, sir, and not good news."

"What does it say?"

"It's from the PM informing Lord Louis that de Gaulle has placed Indo-China within the French Union and instructs him to cancel the meeting."

I read the message to Mountbatten: "De Gaulle declares French Indo-China part of the French Union." In a deeper, sadder voice, the last and devastatingly final word, "Abort", I spoke with anger, in a voice reluctant to say it.

"Now I have to inform Ho. I'll be back when I can," I whispered to Lord Louis, who was as shattered as I.

26

DISTANCE FROM THE Grand Hotel at Siem Riap in Cambodia, to a native dwelling, one in a group of twenty, took but forty minutes on foot. I chose to make the journey in this way so as to prepare my mind for the important things to say to Ho Chi-minh. To go by jeep would have made me obvious.

That my journey should arouse no excitement in the village my uniform, too, was discarded.

The sky was alive with stars and the moon fully awake. Chickens scratched for their supper while pie dogs searched for scraps from the food tables.

No one paid me any attention as I sauntered through the bazaar examining wares displayed on trestle tables illuminated by oil lamps. Had the villagers known of the dire message I was delivering, they would be fearful of their future.

Small groups gathered round musicians playing wind and stringed instruments, giving an atmosphere of theatre to this simple, daily marketplace.

Children played in blissful ignorance of the fate awaiting their homeland.

To them, I was but a Frenchman in baggy pantaloons, wearing a beret and chatting casually in simple French while making a purchase here and there. At each stall I visited I asked, "Ou est la route de Phnom-Penh?"—the arranged password.

At the last stall I was escorted to a pure-white frame-built house with railings picked out in bright yellow.

A figure rose from a wicker chair on the verandah, saying, "Bonsoir, Monsieur, entrée sil-vous plaît." His face was familiar to me for when last I saw him he was wearing the habit of a priest, one of the two decoys who came to the Grand Hotel to deceive watchers into thinking that one of them would be Ho Chi-minh.

I followed him to a beaded curtain covering the open doorway to the house. Graciously he held the beads to one side, making my entry that much easier, then returned to the wicker chair. On guard.

My eyes gradually adjusted to the pale light of a single oil lamp set upon a table in the centre of the small room. A slight figure rose from a chair.

"Bienvenue," said the soft voice of Ho Chi-minh, to which I replied, "Merci, Monsieur," as we had agreed to conduct our discussions in French rather than English for security reasons. To speak English in a native house would attract attention from eavesdroppers.

He invited me to take a seat directly in front of him—so as to be able to see my facial expressions, he explained.

Soon as I was seated, a manservant offered me hot towels from an earthenware bowl with which to freshen my face and hands; a delightful custom of welcome after a journey, no matter how short.

It was to become a long meeting, not by design but for its importance to both Ho Chi-minh and me; both fellow-sufferers needing to let off steam over our disappointment at being thwarted at the last moment. We had built up high hopes of success in persuading national leaders to our plan for preventing civil war in Indo-China by providing a controlled system of independence for the Vietnamese people.

For me, as architect of a scheme to bring together Admiral Mountbatten and Ho Chi-minh in pursuit of this elusive independence, it was essential that I share with Ho Chi-minh some of his bitterness towards the USA and France for unilaterally declaring France as colonial master of Indo China.

I vividly recall much of our long and searching discussion, while my deep and sincere sentiment for this true nationalist and statesman has not diminished over the intervening years.

I remember clearly Ho's first intuitive remark describing his sad acceptance that we'd lost our case, something he'd always feared but dared not mention till now.

I noticed him stroking his flimsy long beard and was reminded that when in disguise he parted the long strands so as to conceal this hirsute feature by spreading it on either side of his face. He had a way of attaching the ends on each side to his ears thereby appearing unshaven but beardless.

Ho was vehement in asserting that history would record the degree of hate the world would bestow upon the USA and France for their brutal and uncaring disregard "for our national sovereignty".

He spoke of how, with his Chinese friends, he had prepared for this outcome.

He was positive that with his allies he would punish "these two pathetic bullies", who would suffer protracted and painful ignominy throughout the battles that would rage from north to south, ending in stalemate when the USA would sue for a shameful armistice.

I saw how from time to time he would pause, as if holding back the tears was painful and causing respiratory problems. I saw, too, how when gripping the arms of his chair so fierce was his resolve his knuckles were white—such was the passion of his anger.

"Are you all right?" I remember feeling compelled to ask when his composure seemed to return. He thanked me and quietly closed his eyes in thought; relaxing.

After resting for five minutes, he clapped his hands and automatically tea was served. We paused for refreshment, including some delicious sweetmeats, after which I was invited to make myself comfortable.

On my return to the room, I was alone, but not for long as Ho returned in his usual high spirits suggesting an interval and a game of chess to take our minds away from politics.

My skill at chess was good enough for my brother officers, in fact better than most. I once won a bet that I could beat the general over three games. The wager was one bottle of scotch for each game. I went down on the first to a brilliant opening gambit but recovered in the next two games, due, I have to admit, to over-ambitious daring of the general by allowing his queen to become too exposed in both games.

I told Ho Chi-minh of this experience and, to my delight, he laughed, asking if I always bet at chess? I told him, "No, not as a rule. This is just what army officers do to relieve monotony, and, of course, when showing off."

Playing chess with Ho Chi-Minh was circumspect. His daring was that of the master leaving me no chance of winning. But he graciously played me again without his queen and one knight on the board, which made a difference but I still couldn't checkmate him.

He was relaxed now and obviously wanted to return to politics.

At this point we were interrupted; a man I took to be a servant came into the room and, speaking in Annamese, said in quiet tones something that pleased Ho Chin-minh, for it caused him to chuckle happily. I had found it so easy to be in sympathy with this dedicated national leader, who'd been cheated by the very people who, with wisdom, could have won his genuine friendship.

From now on Ho retained a genial manner as though a weight had been lifted from him. He explained to me that it was good news about a very dear friend whose wife had produced a fine, big baby boy, thus evincing his simplicity among the problems and burdens of state affairs.

I still hear his deep emotion when speaking of my personal disappointment, which he described as a pain matching his own.

He could tell from the chill my pale countenance brought into the room that my news must be negative; his worst fears had come to pass. So disturbed was he, his anger spilled from his voice as he scathingly referred to the USA as "Mighty 'Merica", his description of a cartoon republic, living in fear of something they know very little about, like a child afraid of the dark.

The tone of voice grew in volume as he expounded

his deepest resolve for the ultimate well-being of his people.

He shared with me some of his strategic plans for defending heritage, customs and religious freedom against a sophisticated Western foe, fully armed with every up-to-date weaponry, including the atomic bomb, already used against the Japanese with massive killing of unarmed civilians. This extreme action, Ho said, exposes another example of fear. When Japan brilliantly planned for and successfully brought about the destruction of America's navy at Pearl Harbor, panic had spread throughout the USA and brought them unreservedly into the war with a vengeance.

Ho spoke of the need for him to use every dirty trick, including some long-forgotten heinous methods which, to Western rules of war, were uncivilised, frightening surprises. He was sure the USA's soft, drafted soldiers dragged from cosy civilian jobs would be unable to cope with these extreme conditions, especially those held in reserve in Bangkok, already demoralised and softened by licentious living, never thinking they would be called into front-line combat.

Finally, he promised, they shall have drugs and venereal diseases. They'll feel the full force of our Chinese and other allies manned by professional, long-serving and ruthless troops, who'll outsmart these American and French rookies. We'll render thousands of them unfit to fight by any means.

His forces will be a phantom army: seldom seen above ground and striking where and when least expected.

No conventional warfare, for this would be to American advantage with their big artillery guns and aerial spotting and bombing. The jungle will hide his troops when forced to break cover for tactical purposes.

He said, with cruel pride, it will be a guerrilla war of such ferocity as never seen before, that will bewilder Western-trained French and American civilian armies.

Ho then became silent. He crossed his hands on his lap and lightly closed his eyes. His head almost imperceptibly nodded.

On opening his eyes, he arose from his chair and lifted something from the table beside him. I sensed we were at the end of our meeting.

He approached me as I stood up, and I heard this charismatic leader of vast numbers of people graciously thanking me for my efforts on behalf of the Vietnamese people to obtain their lawful right to independence.

I was amazed when what he'd taken from the table was placed in my hands, surprising me with its weight.

I opened the package to find a gold cigarette case, which he described as an "inadequate reward' for the dangers I had experienced when abducted by Russian secret agents.

27

IT WAS NEARER 0200 hours when I returned, in pensive mood. Ho's fierce reaction to the cancelling of the meeting and de Gaulle's decision was no shock to me. I had sensed the outcome. I reported the substance of my meeting with Ho Chi-minh to Lord Louis, who listened, surprise clearly showing in his face. "I agree," he said listlessly. "I can't see the French lasting too long in a colonial war, can you?"

"That will depend on who wants France to hang on to Indo-China. Not so much for France's benefit but to prevent Russia spreading to the south. There's only one Western power strong enough, and that's America."

"You can't be serious, Andrew! America is as tired of war as we are."

"Face facts, sir. Who else could do it? And it has to be done or we can say goodbye to Malaya in the long term."

"You mean America will fight with the French against Ho Chi-minh? Actually use American troops? I don't believe it!"

"Not to start with. In the beginning they'll supply military hardware and money—little by little they'll be dragged in as the French falter. It's the age-old game of supplying arms for someone else to do the dirty work so as to achieve the end you want."

"So what you're saying is, America has influenced de Gaulle's decision to take Indo-China back into the French Union?"

"That's what Ho Chi-minh believes, and he's not so wide of the mark, sir. You know, stubborn as he is, de Gaulle had to have support from someone. If not the Americans— who?"

"God knows," Mountbatten replied. "I have to agree, it looks very much like American influence."

"You should hear what Ho thinks about other things. Here is a very strange man. Instead of being angry, or outwardly furious with de Gaulle and others, he was paternal and philosophically understanding; even a little superior, with a touch of the condescending. 'De Gaulle,' he said, 'has made a fatal decision! As has America.' Ho thinks little of our chances from now on, having worked it out that we in the West have gone soft. Our systems, based on democracy and capitalism, without discipline and exacerbated by corruption, he asserts, have inbuilt, self-destructive mechanisms. Democracy is its own time-bomb likely to blow at any time. As for the trade unions, he has no doubt that they will become unmanageable. In fact, aided by international communism, their strength of unity will be such as to bring industrial chaos should they so wish."

"Only history will decide this," said Lord Louis, "and Ho's prognosis sits well with other observers. For this reason we have decided to retain continuous intelligence vigilance in these parts. The Prime Minister has asked me to get your reaction to a proposal that you, Andrew, stay behind when the commission is withdrawn, and provide this flow of information. As we know, the French will find it impossible to restore normal colonial life here. Ho Chi-minh's guerrillas will harass them continually. Obviously China and Russia will provide arms and military advice. As you yourself have said, sooner or later the French will crack under the strain of maintaining a line of communication several thousand miles long. We'll never hear the truth from Paris and it's vital to our interests in Malaya that we know what's going on here. The Americans also need to know but, after Shaw's defection, their OSS's French Indo-China section is under a cloud. You name your price, Andrew, whatever and whoever you want you can have. You'll need to think about it, of course. Naturally, you will not continue as a soldier though you will retain your commission with the rank of full colonel. The PM thought you might become a 'French businessman' in, say, imports and exports, so as to be free to move about and out of the country. How does that strike you, Andrew?"

"Oddly enough," I said, allowing a wry smile to crease one side of my mouth, "it has its appeal. But such a big decision with many ifs and buts. I'll have to return to England before deciding."

"That's understood," agreed Lord Louis. "The PM wishes to discuss it with you in any case. You'd have the fullest MI backing and support. I understand a special section, Secret Intelligence Service, is being formed. By the way, what's happening to Shaw, Ulowski and the French girl?"

"Too soon to say. There may be difficulties with the French regarding Suzie and Eddie Blitz—unless he's remained Dutch. He'd certainly be in trouble had he acquired French nationality."

The Dakota took off into the morning sun and made the long turn while climbing across the low hills.

I watched its graceful rise as the sun's brilliant glint on the windshield flashed and the pilot levelled out, on course for Singapore. I was wondering who could have told de Gaulle of the proposed meeting: it certainly wasn't Suzie—though it was her job to do so! Most likely, I decided, Madame Bastien had informed Admiral d'Argenlieu—she'd had Sergeant Fagge to tell her!

Maryse, Suzie and Blitz stood with me, each speculating on the future. Eddie Blitz was excited and already reshaping his import-export business to meet the new requirement, while the women were trying hard to adjust to the inclusion of the young and very beautiful Marie-Claire in the team.

Once more I recalled Drury's warning that Gracey was pro-French—he was miscast in the job. Now the scene had shifted dramatically and any remaining respect I had for this general vanished—all values now demeaned.

Suddenly, I realised the size of my own responsibilities to my operatives. It hit me with such force, I felt off balance for a while.

Through a fog of confusion Suzie's predicament became paramount. She had violated every trust, every solemn obligation to her country, for an ideal: to avert a tragedy of epic dimensions. I felt responsible for her plight. Though not as assassin of Deshampneuf, it might appear to the French she was an accomplice.

Finally, fear of losing her to possible execution by the French made me realise I was desperately in love with her.

Then I thought of Maryse. Maryse had totally identified with our plan for some degree of independence for Ho Chiminh. As a French woman, I feared she would be treated as a traitor. How could I help her?

My mind now less confused, ideas were forming—God, what a mess I've got these wonderful people into.

Eddie Blitz as a Dutchman: I considered his position and found it unlikely to save him entirely; if nothing else, he'd be deported.

As for Sie-ling, I felt sure a way could be found of getting him out of the country. His family always kept funds abroad.

Marie-Claire was the one shining light, a French heroine. They could make great play of this; her mad, brave and dangerous attempt to prevent Mountbatten and Ho Chiminh meeting could bring her acclaim and highest decorations; but I doubted if the French would make capital out of this, for she was armed with a revolver when attempting to enter Lord Louis's room.

Then, in a flash it came to me. To gamble on pressurising Gracey. I must challenge him in regard to criticisms he'd earned for himself—his shortcomings, and arrogance in exceeding his remit to disarm the Japanese. He'd certainly meddled in politics—and bragged about it!

28

GRACEY CALLED ME in to report. The staggering news I'd had from Stafford about Fagge, and the general's support for French resumption of power, strengthened my hand.

"Do you want it in writing?" I asked, cynically.

"No," the general lazily replied, as though happy with the way things had gone. "You only had one minor incident with Captain Hunter on the way to Siem Riap. No injuries to his men, fortunately. Good show, Andrew." His voice had a cockiness, a gloating... he had, after all, achieved his desire to be influential in restoring the French to power in Vietnam.

Then I told him of the kidnapping and its outcome.

"How many did you kill?" he asked with concern.

"Three, they were Russians. Colonel Grekowski was the leader. A spymaster."

"You've a charmed life, Andrew." He sounded like he wished I hadn't.

The general appeared puzzled, pondering how to deal with the killings.

"Better get Peter Bain in on this one, Andrew." He buzzed the intercom, Bain answered immediately.

Peter Bain was excited, anticipating something juicy about my visit to Siem Riap. He shook my hand wildly, almost hugging me.

"Good to see you safe and well, Andrew. I'd heard unsavoury stories of that Plaine des Jones—very dangerous at times."

I told him briefly of Hunter's incident.

Turning to the general, Bain asked, "What's this tricky problem?"

"Until Andrew told me of his kidnapping and the killing of three Russians—one a colonel—there'd been no need for a written report. Now, I think you and Andrew should discuss the whole affair. Then we can decide what course to take, if any."

This suited me. It gave me the chance to discuss with Bain the plight of my operatives.

"How about tomorrow morning in your office?" said Bain.

"Fine, about 0900," I suggested.

"Agreed. I'm looking forward to it. Sounds exciting."

The rest of the day I spent with my team. We discussed everything. If necessary, I told them, ways could be found to get them out of the country.

"I'm meeting with Peter Bain tomorrow to see if there's a diplomatic problem. In my opinion there's none—the Russians were the aggressors putting my life on the line. We killed them in self-defence," I reassured them.

Peter Bain was as usual warm and cordial and now eager to hear my story first-hand. A strong rapport between us had developed from our first meeting. He took the chair on the other side of my desk.

I related the whole happening from the time of my being accosted to the last shot fired. Bain was surprised to hear of Suzie crawling through the monsoon drain into the powerhouse and shutting down the floodlights.

"Suzie's act of bravery deserves recognition. We can't give it to her, nor can the French. The circumstances cannot be recorded—the whole affair must be a non-event," explained Peter Bain.

"You mean, this terrible happening is to be forgotten?" I asked.

"Yes, Andrew. We're under no obligation to say anything. It never happened as far as we're concerned. Even if they'd killed you, the record would show your death as *killed in action*. The Russians don't want the world to know they kidnapped an ally and threatened to kill him."

My strained apprehensions melted away, my body relaxed, tension almost gone. This was the moment I wanted—to explain my most serious problem to Bain.

"There's one worrying matter we can't wish away," I started. "I need your opinion concerning my non-military operatives—my local civilians, French, Chinese and Dutch. Now the French are in government I fear these agents are at risk."

"Tell me more," Bain invited.

"I've had three civilian agents for about two years performing legitimate acts of intelligence against the Japanese," I explained. "Since the idea of a meeting between Lord Louis and Ho Chi-minh was instigated these three agents have worked actively towards the fruition of our plan: a French woman, a Chinese man and a Dutchman. The Sureté will want to question them about their actions.

"My main concern is the fate of the French woman I've fallen in love with! She's been heavily involved in setting up the meeting between Lord Louis and Ho Chi-minh. This is a serious matter. She's a captain in the French army attached to the Corps Diplomatique. I managed to persuade her of the potential disaster of civil war if the French resumed colonial rule in Indo-China. She became an active supporter of our plan to do a deal with Ho for some form of independence, contrary to the aims of her native country."

"Now we really *do* have a problem of some size," a worried Peter Bain commented.

"I've been wondering," I ventured, "if we can pressure Gracey into enlisting Le Clere's help. You will recall that Gracey was not opposed to the idea of a meeting between Lord Louis and Ho Chi-minh. He'd not like the French to know of this."

Peter Bain looked hard at me. "You are a devious fellow, Andrew. What more's brewing in your cunning brain?"

"Think of the stink the world's press could create if they knew that members of my team are to be punished for attempting to prevent a bloody civil war in this country. The general's name will be linked in taking sides contrary to Lord Louis's orders. They won't want the world to know a French woman armed with a pistol had threatened the life of Admiral Mountbatten. The Yanks won't shine in glory, either! I think, Peter, we've enough justification for asking General Le Clere to forget about it. After all, the French have what they want—Gracey accelerated the French takeover. Magnanimity is, perhaps, the word the French might like to hear."

The diplomat in Peter Bain was hard at work. Although

silent, his brain was in top gear, and his face full of expression, sometimes staring at me quizzically, asking silent questions; sometimes softly smiling. Eventually his smile grew in size. He was suddenly bursting with excitement.

"You've given me the clue to the problem and I've the essential ingredient. It's a secret I can't divulge. Andrew, trust me."

I thought an answer would never come. As the days dragged by, Peter Bain heard nothing. He couldn't easily enquire beyond the general. Bain began to doubt that Gracey had put our case to General Le Clere, such was the low esteem we now had, due to Gracey's very odd behaviour.

Three weeks later, the very day Gracey left the commission, he sent for me and Peter. He told us the matter had been dropped by the French.

My team celebrated throughout the night, rendering us unfit for duty next day. I never asked Peter Bain to reveal his secret weapon that enabled him to put pressure on Gracey, but everything pointed to some highly sensitive information Bain acquired when serving at the British Embassy in Paris before the war.

I wondered who among the leading players in our drama had a very black mark in his or her file! Or was it perhaps someone of much higher rank with more to lose if exposed?

EPILOGUE

THE HOLOCAUST OF "Vietnam"!